The Dew Point

by Neena Beber

A SAMUEL FRENCH ACTING EDITION

FOUNDED 1830

SAMUELFRENCH.COM

ISBN 978-0-573-69662-6   Printed in U.S.A.   #29071

IMPORTANT BILLING AND CREDIT REQUIREMENTS

All producers of *THE DEW POINT must* give credit to the Author of the Play in all programs distributed in connection with performances of the Play, and in all instances in which the title of the Play appears for the purposes of advertising, publicizing or otherwise exploiting the Play and/or a production. The name of the Author *must* appear on a separate line on which no other name appears, immediately following the title and *must* appear in size of type not less than fifty percent of the size of the title type.

In addition the following credit *must* be given in all programs and publicity information distributed in association with this piece:

The Dew Point was presented by Gloucester Stage in 2001
and the Summer Play Festival in 2004.

THE DEW POINT had its world premiere at the Gloucester Stage (Israel Horovitz, Artistic Director) in 2001. The director was Simon Hammerstein, the set designer was Susan E. Sanders, the lighting designer was Dina Gjertsen, the costume designer was Molly Trainer, and the sound designer was Jesse Soursourian. The production stage manager was Nicole Jesson. The cast was as follows:

JACK	Bill Mootes
GRETA	Laura Napoli
PHYLLIS	Marianne Ryan
KAI	Michael Sáenz
MIMI	Emme Shaw

CHARACTERS

MIMI *(30s)*

JACK *(40s)*

PHYLLIS *(30s)*

KAI *(30s)*

GRETA *(early 20s)*

Dedicated to Joyce Sacks Beber and Jennifer I. Beber,
my mother and sister,
my best friends.

ACT 1

Scene One

(Mimi and Kai's apartment. **MIMI** *stares at a chair.* **JACK** *watches her. After a moment,* **MIMI** *sits in the chair. The chair is a design prototype, minimalist, strange and of-the-moment.)*

MIMI. It's comfortable.

JACK. You're surprised?

MIMI. Much more comfortable than it looks.

JACK. It looks uncomfortable?

MIMI. Not *un*-comfortable.

JACK. Because if you don't like it –

MIMI. I like it.

JACK. Do you?

MIMI. I do.

JACK. I want you to love it.

MIMI. It's a great chair, Jack.

JACK. It's a tremendous chair.

MIMI. "Great" and "tremendous" are pretty much interchangeable.

JACK. Not for a gusher. You're a gusher. "Great," well, you've pretty much devalued the word "great" by using it so often.

MIMI. I love the chair.

JACK. It has integrity, this chair. That was important to me: its purity. You think Kai will like it?

MIMI. He'll love it.

JACK. I hope so.

MIMI. That's nice, that you want Kai to like it.

JACK. Sometimes I think he doesn't like me so much.

MIMI. He likes you, Jack.

JACK. Really? Because I like Kai.

MIMI. He thinks it's great that we're friends. I mean not "great." Supreme. He thinks it's supreme.

JACK. I can't believe you're getting married, Meems.

MIMI. I know, neither can I.

JACK. Maybe I should try it.

MIMI. Try it *again*, you mean.

JACK. To say "*again*" would somehow connect a second time with the first time, which I certainly do not want to do.

MIMI. Well you weren't married for very long, were you. A week, wasn't it something like that?

JACK. We got married in order to end it.

MIMI. There's logical.

JACK. I was too young, but now…I think it might be nice. To be done with the craziness. I can see doing it.

MIMI. You and Greta?

JACK. I can see it in the abstract.

MIMI. But it's going well, you and Greta.

JACK. It is. It was. She's been depressed lately. Her career, whatever, a lot of rejection, blah blah. She can't take it.

MIMI. It's tough.

JACK. I can't take it, either. Having to hear about it – do you know what we talk about all the time? Headshots, call-backs, casting agents. I do not want to have another conversation about headshots in my life.

MIMI. I've heard this before.

JACK. I know. You were right. What can I say? You were right about actresses.

MIMI. I had a feeling, though, that this time it might be different. You've seemed happy.

JACK. Frankly she's a little bit boring.

MIMI. Really?

JACK. Let's just say she's not an intellectual. That's okay; she's incredibly bright, but she – I mean she's not well-read. She's – that's not her thing. I just wish she had a little more curiosity. It could be the depression. What did you think?

MIMI. Of Greta?

JACK. What did you think, honestly?

MIMI. I barely met her.

JACK. You spoke after her show.

MIMI. For a minute.

JACK. Don't hold back.

MIMI. I'm not. She seemed nice.

JACK. "Nice"?

MIMI. We exchanged two words. What do you want me to say? She seemed great, okay? Sorry – tremendous. She's tremendous.

JACK. She's very talented.

(MIMI *doesn't say anything.*)

She is, Meems. She's talented. You couldn't tell in that thing.

MIMI. No, no, I thought she was great. In the most superlative sense of the word. Very good.

JACK. She's more of a dancer. That's how she started.

MIMI. That makes sense.

JACK. She's so angry at me lately. That's the problem. She's so fucking angry. All the time. It's her family, you know, how she was raised; she really has a lot of anger about, well, basically everything. Me. Mostly about me. Why do I end up with all these women with major father issues?

MIMI. Gee, I don't know, Jack; because the women you date are twelve?

JACK. She's twenty-four, Meems; that's perfectly respectable. She's not a kid.

(*The telephone rings.* MIMI *lets it ring.*)

MIMI. You're twenty years older than her.

JACK. I don't think that's such an issue.

> *(off phone ringing)*
>
> Screening?

MIMI. I have company.

JACK. Company who hates the way you screen. The age thing is really a big non-issue.

MIMI. That's no longer your prerogative, telling me not to screen.

JACK. Why don't you just pick up?

MIMI. I like to know who it is first. I don't like surprises.

JACK. Get caller ID.

> *(As they continue, the phone picks up; a woman speaks after the pause of the outgoing message, which we don't hear.)*

JACK. Does Kai mind the way you screen?

MIMI. He's never said anything.

JACK. He minds.

PHYLLIS. *(V.O.)* Hi, it's me, Phyllis; are you there?

> *(**MIMI** starts looking for the phone receiver.)*

MIMI. Why should he? I always pick up for him.

JACK. He can't be sure.

PHYLLIS. *(V.O.)* I'm on your block…

JACK. *(off the voice)* She sounds cute.

PHYLLIS. *(V.O.)* I have something to show you…

MIMI. Where is the damn phone?

PHYLLIS. *(V.O.)* Oh, well –

> *(**MIMI** finds the phone and answers it.)*

MIMI. Hi, yeah, I'm here; sorry, I couldn't find the phone.

JACK. You shouldn't pick up in the middle.

MIMI. Sure, you can come up. Jack's here.

JACK. It's terrible the way you pick up in the middle, after the person's gone on for a while…

MIMI. You know, that Jack, yes. Come up. Good.

(**MIMI** *hangs up the phone.*)

JACK. As if you're de*cid*ing, con*sid*ering whether or not you will be *both*ered.

MIMI. Phyllis is coming up.

JACK. Phyllis sounds cute. I'm fond of that name. Does the name fit her?

MIMI. You've met her, Jack.

JACK. When?

MIMI. Suddenly you like the name Phyllis?

JACK. It's a good, solid, old-fashioned name. I went out with a Phyllis once.

MIMI. You've gone out with an everyone once.

JACK. You overestimate me, really, you do.

MIMI. Don't you mean *under*-estimate?

JACK. Phyllis Fromlick. When I was driving a cab. I picked her up, she invited me to her place. So I should say she picked me up. And I remember, I remember she was wearing this fur – jacket –

MIMI. I don't need to hear your war stories, Jack.

JACK. That's what things were like when I was nineteen. Women were fearless. Sex had no down side. I stayed there a week, in her Park Avenue crash pad. Got fired by the cab company. God, people had fun back then.

MIMI. You still seem to manage "fun."

(**JACK** *sits in his chair.*)

JACK. You should fix me up.

MIMI. Who with, my enemies?

JACK. Meems. I'm not like that anymore.

MIMI. You know I adore you, but as a boyfriend?

JACK. I'm an excellent boyfriend.

MIMI. I'm sure Greta would agree, hearing you angling for dates.

JACK. It's not going to work out with Greta.

MIMI. You've just decided?

JACK. I think that in truth she's probably gay.

MIMI. Oh, please, you always think that.

JACK. She won't admit it to herself. She hates men. She does. I seriously think she would be happier with another woman.

MIMI. Most women would be after a stint with you.

JACK. I know you don't mean that. Maybe Kai knows someone for me.

MIMI. You do fine on your own.

JACK. I need to expand the pool.

*(The buzzer buzzes. **MIMI** presses the button to unlock the downstairs door.)*

JACK. What's Phyllis's story?

MIMI. What is this sudden interest in Phyllis, whom you don't even remember meeting?

JACK. I might remember. Where did we meet?

MIMI. New Year's.

JACK. Well I'm sure I was not fully sober. You should have more parties, Meems.

MIMI. You have all kinds of ideas for me.

JACK. I need a grown-up. I need a non-actress. Phyllis isn't an actress?

MIMI. No.

JACK. So what do you think?

(The doorbell rings.)

MIMI. I think you should end it with Greta first.

*(**MIMI** opens the door to **PHYLLIS**.)*

MIMI. Hi. You remember Jack.

PHYLLIS. How are you, Jack?

JACK. Nice to see you again.

PHYLLIS. I hope you don't mind. I was right on your block, so —

MIMI. I'm glad you called. Want something?

PHYLLIS. Just water would be great.

MIMI. There's tea.

PHYLLIS. Tea, then.

MIMI. There's beer.

PHYLLIS. That.

JACK. I'll have a beer.

PHYLLIS. Beer in the middle of the day, how decadent.

JACK. Or German.

(*off* **PHYLLIS**'*s look*)

I went to Berlin for a design festival, the thing shut down for three hours in the afternoon so everyone could go drink beer.

(*As* **MIMI** *passes to the kitchen:*)

MIMI. Jack made me this chair. Isn't it nice?

PHYLLIS. I can't believe you made this.

MIMI. It's an engagement chair.

PHYLLIS. That's very sweet. It's a lovely chair.

(**MIMI** *exits to kitchen.*)

Shouldn't there be two?

JACK. One was a lot of work.

PHYLLIS. It must be amazing to be able to make things, useful things.

JACK. I'm going to miss this chair.

PHYLLIS. You actually built it?

JACK. That's what I do. Well, the prototypes I build myself. I like that part – some people just do it all on paper, or work it out on a tiny scale, but I end up discovering a lot as I go. I think this one came out all right, if I do say so myself –

(**PHYLLIS** *tries out the chair as* **MIMI** *reenters with two bottles of beer.*)

PHYLLIS. Do I have to get engaged to get one of these?

JACK. Yes, you do.

> *(looking her in the eyes a little too directly)*

> To me.

PHYLLIS. Oh, really.

JACK. *(casual again)* If you're interested, you should come by my studio.

> (**MIMI** *breaks in, purposefully interrupting the flirtation.*)

MIMI. Here you go –

PHYLLIS. Thanks, Mimi.

MIMI. *(after a pause)* You guys do know I have to get back to work.

JACK. You love being distracted.

PHYLLIS. She does, it's true; but then she likes to complain about it.

MIMI. As it happens, I have a lot to get done today. I've got to put in a bid on a Charles Dickens, a Howard Hughes, and an Edna St. Vincent Millay.

JACK. I worry there's a fine line between what you do and the autograph hounds.

MIMI. I don't work with autograph hounds. This Dickens is a pretty amazing document, by the way.

JACK. Speaking of selling out, tell her about my tapas bar.

MIMI. It's a love letter – from Dickens – apparently the only letter to his mistress that's survived intact.

JACK. *(while gesturing for **MIMI** to get to the point: him)* That's cool, Meems…

MIMI. It is cool. I've got to authenticate it first, but…Jack designed a tapas bar.

PHYLLIS. That new place – Mimi told me about it. She said it's spectacular.

JACK. "Spectacular"? Thanks, Meems. I just did the bar, though.

PHYLLIS. I'm sure that's the part that's spectacular.

MIMI. You really think I'm like those bottom-feeder autograph hounds?

JACK. I was supposed to do the whole thing, but they ran out of money, got some cheap stools. Crap. I can't tell you how much I hate those crap stools. It kills me to see them next to my bar.

PHYLLIS. I'll have to check it out.

JACK. I'll take you there.

MIMI. The food is awful. Sorry, it is. And I'm interested in history, and authenticity, and documents that have meaning and, and significance as a record of a time, not running around getting some celebrity's autograph.

JACK. I know that, Meems, I was teasing. And you're right about the food. I wish they'd let me do the menu…

(to PHYLLIS)

I'm a good cook, you know.

MIMI. Not that good.

JACK. I'm an excellent cook. You, on the other hand, cannot even make spaghetti.

MIMI. If you're still referring to that *one time* I made a mistake.

JACK. You made a gelatinous heap.

(starting to laugh, remembering)

The way it all stuck together –

MIMI. It was angel hair. It's not my fault that it all coagulated into this one chunk –

JACK. Yes, it's not your fault you cooked spaghetti the thickness of a strand of hair for forty-five minutes.

MIMI. I read the directions on the package.

(trying not to laugh)

It's just that I figured 45 seconds was a typo. What cooks in 45 seconds and not in a microwave?

JACK. She had to cut it out of the pot with a knife, but she still served it – with a flourish even –

MIMI. I could not admit defeat.

JACK. She presents it on this platter, the most disgusting thing I've ever seen in my life:

MIMI/JACK. Spaghett-O-Mold.

(They look at each other with a burst of laughter. They both then look at **PHYLLIS**, *remembering she's there.)*

PHYLLIS. One of those where you had to be there.

JACK. It was amusing at the time.

MIMI. Not at the exact time, but the next day.

JACK. I was amused at the moment of presentation.

MIMI. Well I can make spaghetti now, Jack. Kai loves my spaghetti.

PHYLLIS. Kai's a great cook.

JACK. Kai's a great guy.

PHYLLIS. He is. She's very lucky, our Mimi, she really is.

JACK. Shit, I have to go. I'm running two hours late today.

PHYLLIS. *(eager to leave with him)* I should get going, too.

MIMI. Hey, didn't you want to show me something?

PHYLLIS. Oh, right.

*(***PHYLLIS** *takes a pair of old, cruddy boots out of her bag. She sets them down.)*

PHYLLIS. Stephen Spielberg's shoes.

(They look at them.)

Isn't that funny?

MIMI. Why do you have Stephen Spielberg's old shoes, Phyllis?

PHYLLIS. I was at this shoot –

JACK. You're not an actress…

PHYLLIS. Of course not. Thank you, though. I'm an artist's rep –

MIMI. She works with photographers. A lot of really interesting, um, photographers.

PHYLLIS. One of my guys landed a Spielberg sitting, and Spielberg loved the shoes they had for him – the magazine let him keep them – they had these sickeningly expensive boots and rich people love, love, love getting free stuff, let me tell you. He wanted to walk out in the new ones and he left behind these. Do you think they're worth anything, Mimi?

MIMI. I don't deal in smelly old shoes. Should I get the feeling my work is not much respected by my very dear friends?

PHYLLIS. They're not smelly. They smell quite fresh and powdery.

MIMI. You smelled them?

PHYLLIS. I sniffed.

MIMI. They're stolen goods.

PHYLLIS. I took them from the garbage. Taking things from the garbage is not stealing.

JACK. They have a certain poignancy.

PHYLLIS. You see?

JACK. It's usually new shoes that bring me to tears – a man in shiny new shoes, obviously a little uncomfortable but steppin' out, and when I think of how he picked them out, and put them on in the morning – that sight's always brought me to tears.

(**JACK** *and* **PHYLLIS** *look at each other.*)

MIMI. Aren't you both leaving?

PHYLLIS. *(to* **JACK,** *still focused on him)* You want to have them? Maybe you can incorporate them into a piece.

JACK. Come by my studio, we'll make a trade.

PHYLLIS. Sounds like a plan. Mimi has my numbers.

JACK. Shall I walk you out?

PHYLLIS. I'd never refuse a dashing escort.

(**MIMI** *clears her throat.*)

MIMI. Okay, so, bye bye.

PHYLLIS. Oh, Mimi, I brought you this –

(**PHYLLIS** *reaches into her bag and hands* **MIMI** *a magazine.*)

MIMI. A bridal magazine?

PHYLLIS. I knew you'd be too embarrassed to buy one for

yourself. Time to start planning.

MIMI. I won't be having a "wedding" wedding.

PHYLLIS. That's what they all say at first.

JACK. I'm a firm believer in the Las Vegas chapel. The more Elvis impersonators, the better.

MIMI. Bye, guys.

(*As* **PHYLLIS** *gets her stuff together,* **JACK** *turns to* **MIMI.**)

JACK. (*lowering voice*) She's cute.

MIMI. Okay, yeah.

JACK. I didn't remember her being so cute.

(**PHYLLIS** *comes back over.*)

PHYLLIS. Ready?

MIMI. Thanks again for the chair. And my bridal zine. Thanks.

JACK. Happy engagement, Meems.

PHYLLIS. Yes, happy happy.

(**JACK** *and* **PHYLLIS** *exit.* **PHYLLIS** *pops back in.*)

PHYLLIS. He's adorable, right?

MIMI. I wouldn't have said "adorable," but then –

PHYLLIS. He's not really my type but my type hasn't really worked for me so far, what do you think?

MIMI. I wouldn't have thought, but hey, what do I know –

PHYLLIS. I think he's very adorable. You're okay with it?

MIMI. (*trying, but less than enthusiastic*) Sure.

PHYLLIS. Of course, you're a soon-to-be married woman and I'm a soon-to-be-barren spinster, so why would you care?

MIMI. (*mustering more enthusiasm*) Go for it, Phil.

JACK. (*off-stage, calling up*) Have I lost you?

PHYLLIS. (*calling down*) Coming!

(*to* **MIMI**)

You never know, right?

(**PHYLLIS** *exits.* **MIMI** *sits in the chair and looks out. She picks up one of the bridal magazines, looks at it, then looks back up and out, not sure what to think.*)

Scene Two

*(**MIMI** and **KAI**'s apartment. **KAI** has just entered. He is taking off his jacket or coat. **MIMI** trails him as he puts stuff down.)*

MIMI. Do you think I should have warned her?

KAI. I'm sure she knows. He's an obvious rogue.

MIMI. A "rogue"? Is that still a word?

KAI. I didn't know words went out of business. They're both grown-ups, Meem.

MIMI. He's a womanizer. A major out-of-control womanizer.

KAI. Maybe Phyllis isn't looking for a lasting momentous this-is-it thing.

MIMI. Oh, I happen to know that Phyllis *is* looking for a lasting momentous this-is-it thing.

KAI. Then in the meantime, she can enjoy herself.

MIMI. And maybe he's changed. It's possible, right? I can see that he really wants to change. I think. And maybe he has. Because one never knows. Right? Just because he was a certain way with me – and his history – well I'd hate to be judged from my ancient history. Maybe he just hasn't found the one yet and what if she is the one, you know?

KAI. Can we stop talking about Jack?

MIMI. It's not Jack, it's Phyllis. I know what she's going through. Even if you don't buy into the whole marriage thing, there's this constant pressure to couple.

KAI. What is this?

MIMI. Oh, that's what Jack brought over. Our engagement present.

(beat)

You don't like it?

KAI. Just one?

MIMI. He made it for both of us.

KAI. Did he.

MIMI. I like it. You don't like it?

KAI. You don't *really* like it.

MIMI. I do, Kai.

KAI. It looks uncomfortable.

MIMI. Try it.

KAI. It's your chair.

MIMI. It's for both of us.

KAI. A chair is not a present for two people. A couch, maybe; a love seat.

MIMI. I'm telling you, he really wanted you to like it.

KAI. Well I'm sorry; it doesn't speak to me. It's obviously a one-person chair.

MIMI. I think it can fit two people very nicely.

(**MIMI** *positions* **KAI** *on the chair and climbs onto him.*)

KAI. Oh. Okay now. This is so kinky. Making love with my fiancée on her ex-boyfriend's chair.

MIMI. I hate that word.

KAI. Ex-boyfriend? Chair? I know: kinky.

MIMI. "Fiancée." Sounds dated. Makes me feel dated.

(*The phone rings.* **KAI** *goes to answer it.*)

MIMI. Don't pick up. You don't mind that I screen, do you?

KAI. Everyone who still has a land line screens.

MIMI. That's what I said.

PHYLLIS. *(V.O.)* Mimi? You there? I'm not calling too late, am I? I just want to know what you think about Jack –

KAI. Go ahead.

PHYLLIS. *(V.O.)* He's sexy, right? Am I crazy?

MIMI. *(looking for the phone)* Where is that thing?

(**KAI** *finds the phone and hands it to* **MIMI.** *She shakes her head, smiles at him.*)

PHYLLIS. *(V.O.)* Tell me if I'm –

(**MIMI** *clicks on. As she talks,* **KAI** *finds the bridal magazine and starts to flip through it with increasing shocked bemusement.*)

MIMI. You like him? Yeah? Well obviously at one time I found him to be – no, if you like him – please, it's fine with me. You don't need my permission. What does Kai think? I don't know. What do you think, Kai?

KAI. I think this chair was a lot more comfortable when you were on it with me.

MIMI. He says go for it. Call me in the morning. Okay.

(**MIMI** *hangs up the phone.*)

MIMI. It's not like she needs my permission.

(**MIMI** *goes back to* **KAI**. *He holds out the bridal magazine.*)

KAI. (*reading cover headlines*) "Think Pink: Our Sweetest Bouquets for Spring"; or, wait, this is good, "Carribean Spice: Make Your Honeymoon Both Naughty and Nice."

MIMI. I did not buy that.

KAI. It's okay, really. What else do you keep from me? Pretending to not want a "wedding" wedding – other skeletons in the closet? Barbie dolls? Betty Crocker recipe books?

MIMI. It's not funny, Kai.

KAI. Look at this, a bonus 6-foot fold-out wedding planner!

(**MIMI** *doesn't laugh at the teasing.*)

We do have a wedding to plan.

MIMI. Yes, do we take a cab, bus or subway to City Hall?

KAI. That sounds festive.

MIMI. Okay, horse-drawn coach.

(*beat*)

I never had that whole wedding fantasy. You know that.

KAI. Our first date was a wedding.

MIMI. That was grotesque. I can't believe we survived that.

KAI. "Grotesque" is harsh.

MIMI. And anyway our first date was at the gallery.

KAI. You count that as a date?

MIMI. Tell me how it went – from the beginning.

KAI. You want me to tell you how we met?

MIMI. It's our story. I like having a story.

KAI. Tom said I have this friend who sells old documents – pieces of history – you should meet her; I have this feeling you would like her.

MIMI. And we were supposed to meet at his wedding.

KAI. But then I happened to be passing by that gallery – I was – I thought oh, that's the place he mentioned, why don't I just –

MIMI. In case you wanted to request getting seated at a far-away table.

KAI. I don't know what made me stop by. It was very unlike me.

MIMI. You needed a gift. Your old professor –

KAI. I was improvising.

　　(*beat*)

You didn't know that?

MIMI. No. I thought I'd failed you when you didn't buy anything. Why didn't you tell me that was a lie?

KAI. I would have bought him something, but I couldn't believe how expensive all those pieces of paper were. I almost bought that Polar Explorer's cancelled check, just because it was by far the cheapest thing in the place.

MIMI. Richard E. Byrd.

KAI. A few hundred bucks for someone else's somehow-never-tossed-out garbage, I couldn't do it.

MIMI. And it wasn't just some cancelled check, it was the one he wrote for the supplies on his first expedition.

KAI. So you mean it was a check for toilet paper, wool socks, and long underwear? Okay then, not garbage at all.

MIMI. You could have had a note from Joan Crawford for about the same price.

KAI. Or Thomas Edison's grocery list for what, a couple hundred thousand?

MIMI. I think you're thinking of Bach. I've never had an Edison for more than twenty grand.

KAI. I'll never understand how you price things – Elvis is less than Marilyn Monroe but more than General Patton, on the basis of what?

MIMI. Desire.

KAI. Two million for a Jack Kerouac manuscript when you can just buy the damn book – why two million?

MIMI. It has a value. It's a record of a very important moment in cultural and literary history.

KAI. But why not one million? Or for that matter, three million? One point five? Why two?

MIMI. It's whatever people are willing to pay.

KAI. But you make a determination.

MIMI. Based on availability, historical significance, the quality of the document, the content…Right now, I have a client who wants me to bid on a Dickens letter, up to fifty grand. And if it's authentic, I have a feeling it'll go for even more than that.

KAI. If it were me, I'd keep my fifty grand and settle for a Xerox copy.

(**MIMI** *takes out papers to show* **KAI***; she has a facsimile of the letter.*)

MIMI. It's a letter to the woman he had an affair with for 13 years – he was probably the most famous man in England but he somehow kept the whole thing secret, all their letters were destroyed…but now this one's surfaced. You don't think there's value here?

KAI. It's just very ephemeral, the value you place on something you can't eat, can't wear, and that only debatably looks better on the wall than a flat-screen TV.

(**MIMI** *puts away the papers carefully, turns to* **KAI***.*)

MIMI. Let's go to bed.

KAI. You like it when I give you a hard time. Or – is it the chair.

(*MIMI and* KAI *cross toward the bedroom together.*)

(*Lights shift. A time interlude. It's the middle of the night.* MIMI *comes back out. She goes to her desk and sorts through papers. She looks up.* JACK *is now sitting in the chair.*)

JACK. Hi.

MIMI. (*tentative*) Hi?

JACK. (*grinning*) Come here often?

(*beat*)

It's a great library. This room – I love this room. Early 20th century. It's Beaux-Arts but there's a pared-down simplicity – I find it very modern.

MIMI. Especially the computers.

JACK. Yeah, well, I come here for the furniture.

MIMI. Okay.

JACK. That's what I do. Furniture design. Don't tell me you're here for the books?

(*off* MIMI*'s laugh*)

So have a lemonade with me and tell me about what you're reading.

MIMI. I'm not interested in the books, either. I'm looking at how these were printed.

JACK. So we're both equally…superficial?

MIMI. Right. Judging books by covers is my specialty.

JACK. And?

MIMI. And… I haven't made up my mind yet?

JACK. And it's hot out. And lemonade is very refreshing, I find. And too innocent an offer to refuse, don't you think?

(*She offers a slight smile.*)

I'm Jack.

MIMI. Mimi.

JACK. Mimi, as in La Bohème?

MIMI. I hope not.

(He laughs.)

JACK. You know, Mimi, you and I, we're going to look back
on this someday.

MIMI. Oh?

JACK. It's going to be the story of how we met.

MIMI. And you think that's going to amount to something ?

JACK. I do have a feeling.

MIMI. And let me guess – you always trust your feelings.

*(He reaches out to her but disappears back into darkness
as **KAI** enters. Lights shift.)*

KAI. Mimi?

*(**JACK** is gone. Flashback over. **MIMI** startles.)*

MIMI. You snuck up on me.

KAI. It's 2 in the morning. Come back to bed.

MIMI. I can't get to sleep.

KAI. Even better. Come.

MIMI. *(as they start to go off)* Promise me.

KAI. Promise you what?

MIMI. Promise me we won't become one of those boring,
smug, staid, sexless, complacent, upstanding married
couples, okay?

KAI. I was okay with it until "upstanding."

MIMI. You have to promise, promise me marriage won't
turn us into married people, okay?

Scene Three

(JACK *and* PHYLLIS *at his studio.*)

JACK. I like being true to a world, even if it's not the world we're accustomed to. There are certain things we can't change; the repercussions of gravity, obviously. But maybe we can twist it, defy it, call attention to that defiance, God the truth is I just want to look at you.

PHYLLIS. I can't believe it's so late.

JACK. You're such a beautiful woman.

PHYLLIS. That is so not true.

(checking her watch)

I should go, this night went so fast but I have work in the morning...

JACK. I like your watch.

PHYLLIS. This?

JACK. I'll admit that I said that so I could touch your wrist. Not that it isn't a nice watch.

PHYLLIS. It was cheap. It's a fake. The woman who sells them to me could go to jail. I guess I could go to jail, too. I'm addicted to cheap, fake watches and fake bags. You want me to get you one of these?

JACK. You have beautiful wrist bones.

PHYLLIS. Please, I do not. Really?

JACK. I did a series based on bones. Tables, chairs, beds with joints like wrist bones and ankle bones.

PHYLLIS. I've never thought about my wrist bones.

JACK. Delicate and pronounced. That's an extremely sexy dichotomy.

PHYLLIS. I see.

JACK. *(moving her wrist around)* It's an amazing joint – the way it bends and turns –

PHYLLIS. Are you trying to seduce me, Jack?

JACK. Definitely.

(PHYLLIS *momentarily pulls away.*)

PHYLLIS. Why did it end between you and Mimi?

JACK. *(pulling back, uncomfortable)* She must have gone over that topic.

PHYLLIS. I was living in London at the time.

JACK. What were you doing in London?

PHYLLIS. Going to parties.

JACK. That sounds like a calling.

PHYLLIS. I got it out of my system.

JACK. So who funded the party era?

PHYLLIS. I was a bartender at an American place and by a fluke I got a job working for Christie's. Dated a lot of rich jerks who pray upon auction house girls, most heinously a rich jerk I nicknamed The Germ. I was dating The Germ and she was dating The Sculptor.

JACK. Who was The Sculptor?

PHYLLIS. Didn't you start that way?

JACK. I always did both, really. The furniture and the sculpture. I still do.

PHYLLIS. I remember I was a little jealous.

JACK. Of – ?

PHYLLIS. I liked the idea of you.

JACK. Reality can be crushing.

PHYLLIS. I'd seen some of your work. Mimi told me about it – some pictures in a magazine. I thought, Mimi is dating an artist, a guy who does stuff with his hands – you know what a turn-on that is – and meanwhile I am dating a repressed non-productive weak-chinned inbred germ.

JACK. What happened to The Germ?

PHYLLIS. He found an heiress. The rich like to stick together, ultimately.

JACK. You'd think they'd feel more of an obligation to spread the wealth.

PHYLLIS. Yes, whatever happened to noblesse oblige? But I was hoping you were rich.

JACK. Unfortunately we were always the poor relations. My father was treated like this lug, this day-labor lug, and yet he wrote poetry – no one knew that about him. I found the poems after he died, all neatly copied down in this little dimestore notebook. He'd folded up a couple of form rejections from *The New Yorker*, too. It blew my mind, that my father had been sending poems to *The New Yorker*. He would take out volumes from the library: e. e. cummings, Wallace Stevens, Roethke. Carl Sandburg, I remember the cracked blue spine – My father was this poet, yet because he had no money, he was treated like crap. And I've still got this hatred, this little-boy hatred for people who never have to struggle, who have no idea…

(**JACK** *leans in to kiss* **PHYLLIS**. *She pulls back.*)

PHYLLIS. And yet you must recognize the marquee value.

JACK. Excuse me?

PHYLLIS. People eat that stuff up. Women especially.

JACK. So you're going to make me dig deeper into my usual bag of tricks to win you over?

PHYLLIS. I'm sure you've got something rustling around down there that doesn't come with directions a 2-year-old could follow.

JACK. You're good. Mean, but good.

PHYLLIS. So why did it end? You and Mimi?

JACK. Why does that interest you so much?

PHYLLIS. I'm curious.

JACK. It ran its course. It wasn't meant to be. We're better as friends.

PHYLLIS. No energy there?

JACK. God no, we're like siblings.

PHYLLIS. And that's why it ended?

JACK. Who can remember, it was so long ago. What did Mimi say?

PHYLLIS. She never really said.

JACK. She must have said something. Not too much, I hope.

PHYLLIS. Well exactly. You know Mimi, she keeps that stuff close to the vest.

JACK. Endings are never very understandable, do you think? It's usually a slow corrosion – even the ones that end with a bang, there's usually a gradual decay, preceding.

PHYLLIS. I don't know, I wouldn't stick out decay. I'm a firm believer in cutting one's losses.

JACK. I appreciate that. I doubt I was the easiest guy to be with back then.

PHYLLIS. And now?

JACK. Now let's get back to your wrists.

PHYLLIS. You should make a chair for me.

JACK. I would love to make a chair for you.

PHYLLIS. Do you have chair models, for the dimensions?

JACK. Yes, I'm going to need to study the contours of your – backside – very thoroughly.

PHYLLIS. You'd be terrible for me, I can tell.

JACK. Why do you say that?

PHYLLIS. You have that quality – that bad boy thing.

JACK. Why do people say that?

PHYLLIS. Unfortunately it's a quality I really go for.

JACK. I won't argue with it, then.

(He kisses her. Continues to.)

PHYLLIS. We shouldn't be kissing yet.
We won't go further.
Match.com advises against it.
Not that you're a Match.com kind of guy, but nonetheless –
I'd like to have a child within the next two years.
Have I turned you off yet?

JACK. Hunh uh.

PHYLLIS. I'm very conventional in my wants, in my aspirations.

JACK. I don't think so.

PHYLLIS. No?

JACK. You're an artist.

PHYLLIS. You say that because – ?

JACK. I can tell about people.

PHYLLIS. I am not an artist. I represent artists. Commercial artists.

JACK. Something drew you to it.

PHYLLIS. To being commercial?

JACK. To facilitating the creativity of others. I'm willing to bet you take photographs yourself.

PHYLLIS. Snapshots. When I travel. At birthdays.

JACK. My guess is that you're very good at it.

PHYLLIS. I use a disposable cardboard camera.

JACK. I love cardboard cameras. I remember making one when I was a kid, those pinhole things...how amazing that light can leave an imprint of the world. We should make one of those cameras together – explore the city and take pictures together – I would like to do that with you.

PHYLLIS. When are you going to make me my chair?

JACK. You really like my chairs?

PHYLLIS. Very much.

JACK. Then I'm going to make all my chairs for you, for the rest of my life.

Scene Four

(MIMI and KAI's apartment. PHYLLIS is there. They are having drinks and hors-d'oeuvre.)

PHYLLIS. For the rest of his life. Everything he makes.

MIMI. Really? He said that?

PHYLLIS. It's so romantic, right?

MIMI. I can't believe he said that already.

PHYLLIS. He said that on our first date.

MIMI. He does tend to come on strong.

PHYLLIS. What does that mean?

MIMI. He sounds crazy about you; I'm just saying he comes on strong.

PHYLLIS. What, did he say something like that to you? Is this, like, one of his lines?

MIMI. No. No, not at all.

PHYLLIS. He's working on a chair for me now.

MIMI. Wow. Already?

PHYLLIS. Okay, I always wanted a rock song dedicated to me, but a chair's a start. I like the idea of being a chair muse.

KAI. *(entering from kitchen)* What do you think of "our" chair, Phyllis?

PHYLLIS. It's lovely. Mine's going to be better, though.

MIMI. It took him ten years to make a chair for me.

KAI. For us.

(KAI sets down drinks and a tray with dip.)

Maybe he'd like to give you Mimi's chair.

MIMI. Our chair.

PHYLLIS. Do you think it's a bad sign, Kai? That he's coming on strong? Mmm, good dip.

KAI. Olive tapenade. Probably. I came on strong with Mimi and look where we wound up.

PHYLLIS. Meems is very lucky, our Meems.

MIMI. Meems is very hungry. I forgot how late Jack always is.

PHYLLIS. Really? He's been very prompt.

KAI. He must really like you. Try the dip, Meem.

PHYLLIS. How crazy is this? He's so not who I pictured myself with.

KAI. Who did you picture yourself with?

PHYLLIS. A suit-wearer like you, Kai.

KAI. I'm not a suit wearer.

MIMI. You do wear a suit every day, Kai.

KAI. I refuse to think of myself as a suit wearer. Underneath my suit, I wear a – a cape.

PHYLLIS. I can't believe it's been three weeks. Three weeks is my longest stretch in, in years.

MIMI. The thing is, marriage – everyone makes such a big deal about marriage. It's too much pressure when you should be enjoying dating.

PHYLLIS. It's not marriage, it's finding someone. Finding someone who you can stand. Most people, after a while, well it's hard to find someone who doesn't bug the shit out of you, don't you think?

KAI. Can I re-fill?

PHYLLIS. *(nodding "yes")* And I want children. That's the reality. That's the biology of it. It gets desperate and it gets ugly and the men out there, frankly, the men of our generation suck. Not you, Kai.

(KAI takes her glass.)

Don't let me get drunk.

(KAI exits.)

PHYLLIS. There are of course exceptions. He's genius sexy.

MIMI. I know, I lucked out.

PHYLLIS. Not Kai. I mean yes, Kai's great, but Jack, Jack is extremely, extremely sexy. I waited a week and then, God, it was maybe the hottest sex in, like – he's totally hot. You never told me that.

MIMI. You know I don't think I really like thinking about it. It's too weird.

PHYLLIS. Oh, okay.

MIMI. I mean we were together for a *while*.

PHYLLIS. I'm sorry. I thought because it was so long ago –

MIMI. I think it's great. It's just weird to hear details. Don't get too graphic, okay?

PHYLLIS. No problem. He said you guys were much better as friends.

MIMI. Yes, that's true.

(*bothered*) He said that?

PHYLLIS. He said he'd design bookcases for me, too. You know, for all my over-sized photo books. I can't believe he can make stuff. I guy who can make stuff, shelves, that's just – hot. Should I not call him hot?

MIMI. Next you'll be telling me he has nice "buns."

PHYLLIS. He does. Don't you remember?

MIMI. No. I've blocked all that out and I'd like to continue to do so.

PHYLLIS. I'm going to help him get his furniture placed in some photo spreads. We're always looking for stuff.

MIMI. Jack will be grateful, I'm sure.

(*a long pause*)

PHYLLIS. Kai seems well. He works like a dog, doesn't he.

MIMI. I'm not sure if we should get married.

PHYLLIS. What?

MIMI. I mean I want to marry Kai, that's not the issue, but I suddenly realized, all this pressure to get married – why? Why do we have to get married? Maybe if we have children…

PHYLLIS. Of course you'll have children.

MIMI. Why is that an "of course"?

PHYLLIS. Mimi, face it, you are not some radical boho chick. You found yourself a nice lawyer – a lawyer who can cook, even – now it's time to get hitched and make babies and have a wonderful time furnishing a country home together.

MIMI. Jesus, write me the end of my life in 30 seconds or less.

PHYLLIS. Meems, don't whine about your good fortune, it isn't nice.

(KAI *enters with a pitcher and glasses on a tray.*)

KAI. I made mojitos.

MIMI. Yum; Kai makes a damn fine mojito.

(*The phone rings.*)

MIMI. Ignore that.

PHYLLIS. It might be Jack.

(MIMI *and* KAI *look for the phone;* KAI *finds it and starts to pick up.*)

MIMI. Screen, Kai; Jack hates being screened, I'm proving a point.

(*A woman's voice:*)

GRETA. *(V.O.)* Hello, um, this is Greta, I'm actually looking for –

(MIMI *grabs the phone just in time. She speaks into the phone, bringing it away from* PHYLLIS *and* KAI.)

MIMI. Hello?

(PHYLLIS *sips her drink.*)

PHYLLIS. So what constitutes a mojito?

MIMI. Oh. I see.

KAI. Rum, sugar, lime, mint. That's it.

MIMI. Yes, he should be.

PHYLLIS. It works. I see drunkenness at the end of this glass.

MIMI. I will. Tell him.

KAI. The proportions are key. Plus good rum.

MIMI. Certainly. Right.

KAI. It's Cuban. You've never had one?

MIMI. Oh, no problem. Right. Take care.

(**MIMI** *hangs up the phone.*)

PHYLLIS. Who was that, Meems?

MIMI. Sorry, work thing.

KAI. On a Saturday night?

MIMI. I really need to put in a separate line…
She was calling from London.

KAI. Isn't it 3 in the morning there?

MIMI. Did I say *from* London? *For* London. She has a client
over there who collects Prime Ministers. She heard I
had a postcard from Winston Churchill.

(*The buzzer buzzes.*)

There he is. Someone, sit in his chair.

PHYLLIS. I will.

MIMI. Kai, you should. He thinks Kai hates his chair.

KAI. I do.

MIMI. Come on, Kai, be gracious.

KAI. (*as he sits in it*) Tell me, Phyllis, is a chair for one a
proper gift for two?

PHYLLIS. I've always thought that when two people marry,
they become one. So one chair is a very poetic, meta-
phorical gift. This stuff is very strong.

KAI. Is it too strong?

PHYLLIS. I like the mint.

(**MIMI** *opens the door to* **JACK.**)

JACK. I'm late. I'm an idiot.

MIMI. We know that, Jack.

PHYLLIS. Have a mojito.

JACK. I apologize, a crisis at the studio – Hi, Sweetie.

(**JACK** *gives* **PHYLLIS** *a kiss.*)

PHYLLIS. Try it. Minty good.

KAI. Thank you; the mint is fresh, you know.

(**KAI** *starts to get up, sits back down.*)

I'm enjoying your chair, Jack.

(KAI now stands and shakes JACK's hand.)

JACK. Hello, Sir.

KAI. Mojito?

JACK. Sounds fine. Cuban theme night?

KAI. No, the theme is mint. I had some extra...

JACK. You did the cooking? Thank God.

MIMI. That isn't funny, Jack.

JACK. Why should you care about being good at something you have no interest in being good at?

KAI. Mimi likes to be good at everything.

(off her look)

And I think she is.

PHYLLIS. *(British accent)* Mimi's bloody perfect.

(They look at her; she shrugs, now without accent.)

She is.

(JACK takes a cassette tape from his pocket and hands it to MIMI.)

JACK. For the hostess. I figured music lasts longer than roses, wine or chocolate.

(MIMI reads the hand-scrawled label on the tape:)

MIMI. "Jack's Blues Shit."

JACK. *(taking out another tape)* I made one for you, too, Sweetie.

KAI. Once again I'm left in the cold.

MIMI. Now, now, I'm very good at sharing.

JACK. It's for you, too, Kai. I put some wonderful stuff on there: Blind Willie McTell, Howlin' Wolf – you like those guys?

KAI. I don't rightly know. Let's put it on.

(The telephone rings. MIMI grabs it.)

MIMI. Hello. No, that's all right.

(looking toward JACK, who is giving the tape to PHYLLIS)

Um, no. I will do, I promise. Okay?

PHYLLIS. *(reading her label)* "Blues Lover – " I won't read the rest. Out loud.

MIMI. It's just a little crazy here now. Bye-bye.

*(**MIMI** hangs up the phone.)*

KAI. London again?

*(**MIMI** gives him a look.)*

MIMI. Would anybody like to see this Charles Dickens letter? Very interesting. Written to Ellen Ternan. His mistress. And it's explicit, too. It does away with the question of did they or didn't they. See, she'd been an actress – she was only 18 when she met him, and he was 45. He basically bought her a cottage and hid her away until he died 13 years later, denied the whole thing to the end.

KAI. I'll get the food ready.

JACK. Why don't you put on my tape?

MIMI. We don't have a cassette player.

KAI. Don't we have that boom box?

MIMI. When I finally switched to CDs, I was like the last, I did an outdated-technology purge.

KAI. Wait, I have one somewhere, I think.

*(**MIMI** exits to the bedroom, **KAI** to the kitchen.)*

JACK. Nothing compares to vinyl. Oh, God, listen to me, what a cliché. But I'm one of those. I like hearing the scratches. The grooves. The rawness. I hate the digital sound, the way they smooth out all the rough edges.

PHYLLIS. You know what I think was the best? Eight-track tapes. I think it's tragic that I missed out on eight-track tapes. My best friend in elementary school had this much older sister and that's what she listened to. Big chunky things.

*(**JACK** kisses her.)*

JACK. You look delicious.

PHYLLIS. I do?

JACK. Sorry I was late.

PHYLLIS. I never drink, so when I drink, it goes straight to my head.

JACK. I'll get you home safely, little girl.

PHYLLIS. Should I trust you?

JACK. Absolutely not.

(The telephone rings. PHYLLIS *and* JACK *are absorbed in each other. As* GRETA *speaks,* JACK *and* PHYLLIS *pull apart.* JACK *jumps up.)*

GRETA. *(V.O.)* Hello? Sorry, it's Greta again, I'm looking for Jack...

*(*MIMI *walks in from one side carrying a Walkman with a headset.* KAI *walks in from the other side carrying a casserole dish.* MIMI *goes for the phone...)*

GRETA. *(V.O.)* He left his watch here and I really need to –

*(*JACK *grabs the phone before* MIMI *can get to it.)*

JACK. *(into phone)* What are you doing?

MIMI. I should really get rid of that ancient phone machine –

JACK. You can't do this. I'm with my friends. I'll talk to you later, okay? I can't. I'm sorry, I can't do this. I can't.

*(*JACK *hangs up the phone. There is a long pause.* KAI *has entered with the food,* MIMI *with a Walkman.)*

KAI. It's kind of a variation on a Moroccan chicken with couscous. Lots of mint.

MIMI. *(showing Walkman)* This is all I could find for the tape.

PHYLLIS. *(falsely cheery, head spinning)* London called again.

(a pause)

MIMI. I'll, um, I'll just go ahead and...

*(*MIMI *gets the tape for the Walkman.)*

PHYLLIS. I think I'm feeling a little sick.

*(*PHYLLIS *goes to lean back on the couch.* MIMI *puts the cassette into the Walkman. During the following she places it on the coffee table and kneels behind it, trying to turn out the earphones to make speakers.)*

PHYLLIS. What did London want, Jack?

(*JACK goes to* **PHYLLIS**.)

JACK. I'm sorry. I have a crazy ex-girlfriend. I told you about Greta; she's kind of stalking me right now.

KAI. *(to the room; no one's listening)* Uh, dinner's way past ready.

JACK. I didn't want to tell you I was there because she was threatening suicide.

(**PHYLLIS** *lies back, her head spinning.*)

PHYLLIS. That's – awful.

JACK. I had to go.

PHYLLIS. Is she all right?

JACK. I waited for her best friend to come over. I had to wait and make sure she'd be all right.

PHYLLIS. How awful. How really, really awful.

JACK. I shouldn't be responsible, but what could I do?

MIMI. Sshhh…Listen…

(**JACK** *sits beside* **PHYLLIS**, *holding her.*)

JACK. Don't worry, Sweetie.

PHYLLIS. I think I have to lie down for a second.

(**PHYLLIS** *stretches out on the couch.*)

JACK. Close your eyes; there you go.

(**JACK** *strokes* **PHYLLIS** ' *hair.*)

MIMI. Guys? Hear it? If you really listen, you can hear it coming through the headphones.

KAI. That's not an ideal way to listen to music, Meem.

MIMI. *(to herself, as she tunes out the others)* I think it suits it. Sort of hushed and tinny and you have to work at it… and tune everything else out…you know?

(**KAI** *comes and kneels beside* **MIMI**. *They share the head-set, each turning one earphone toward an ear, coming closer as they hold the separate earphones to an ear, ignoring* **JACK** *and* **PHYLLIS** *behind them. As the lights fade out the music comes up and we hear it full-blast, a blues song that wails.*)

Scene Five

(Early the next morning; MIMI *is settling down to work. A light tapping at the door. She doesn't hear it as she finishes a mug of tea, goes to her desk. The tapping grows louder and more rhythmic. She looks through the peephole.)*

MIMI. Hello? Oh.

*(*MIMI *opens the door,* GRETA *enters.)*

GRETA. Hi.

MIMI. Greta.

GRETA. Sorry I didn't call first.

*(*MIMI *looks at her, waiting. An awkward pause.)*

Can I have something to drink?

MIMI. Sure. A glass of water?

(pointedly) Milk?

GRETA. Do you have orange juice?

MIMI. We might.

*(*MIMI *starts for the kitchen.)*

GRETA. "We might." That's nice. To be able to say that.

MIMI. What?

GRETA. That must be nice, to be a "we."

MIMI. Just orange juice, then?

GRETA. Yeah. Just juice.

*(*MIMI *exits to the kitchen.* GRETA *looks around. Picks up a photo or two. Picks up the cassette tape, reads the label, puts it back down. Sees the chair. Sits on it.* MIMI *comes back with a half-full glass of orange juice.)*

MIMI. This is all we have left. I have left.

GRETA. Thanks. I'm addicted to orange juice. I fucking love it lately. I don't know why that is. I go through these phases, like sometimes, sometimes I just need to have this particular ingredient, for like, weeks. I was on yogurt for a while. I was on bologna for an entire month. Bologna sandwiches. I just had to have 'em. And I'm a vegetarian.

(**MIMI** *looks at her, not sure what to say.*)

MIMI. I'm actually about to get to work, I've got a ton to do today so –

GRETA. This is Jack's chair.

MIMI. He made it, yes.

(*pause*)

GRETA. It's not very comfortable.

(*tiny pause*)

MIMI. Kai doesn't think so, either. It was an engagement present. Kai is my – the one to whom I am engaged.

GRETA. This is a nice place.

MIMI. Thank you.

GRETA. I like the way you've got it.

MIMI. Thanks. It's still kind of hodge-podge, but, you know.

GRETA. You've got nice stuff.

(*pause*)

MIMI. So what's up, Greta?

GRETA. Is it mostly yours or his?

MIMI. It's both of ours. It's a mixture. We got some of it together.

GRETA. You work at home?

MIMI. Yes, Greta, which is why it's kind of difficult to begin my day sometimes so if you'll please –

GRETA. Why am I here?

MIMI. It's nice to see you, but I'm trying to get to work, actually, so yes, perhaps – you should tell me, yes, the reason you came here.

GRETA. I want to know the truth.

MIMI. The truth?

GRETA. I want to know. Are you sleeping with Jack?

MIMI. Am I *what*?

GRETA. I have a right to know.

MIMI. Jesus.

GRETA. What is going on between the two of you?

MIMI. Nothing is going on. I am not sleeping with Jack, no.

GRETA. Why does he come here?

MIMI. We're friends.

GRETA. He comes here, he makes you *tapes*. What the fuck is that? He makes you a chair.

MIMI. The chair is for me and my – my fiancé, God I hate that word, "fiancé."

GRETA. He comes here frequently. He never brings me.

MIMI. It's not that social.

GRETA. I don't get what that means.

MIMI. I can assure you, Greta –

GRETA. You were together a long time.

MIMI. Before you were born.

GRETA. That's very patronizing.

MIMI. I'm sorry.

GRETA. Is it because I'm younger or because I'm an actress slash dancer that people frequently patronize me?

MIMI. I don't mean to patronize you.

GRETA. I'm aware of the humiliation of the slash. I'm aware that the thing that I do is a source of jokes told at my expense. That the way I express myself – through my body – what I like to do – is a joke to people.

(A pause; MIMI takes a cookie form the bag and eats it.)

GRETA. Jack believes in me and he makes me better. I'm a better person when I'm with him. And I know he loves me, and I love him better than anyone else can, and if you're still fucking him, what the hell is that?

MIMI. I'm engaged, for Christ's sake. I'm very happily with someone else.

GRETA. In that case, what are you doing hanging out with your ex-lover, letting him give you gifts, calling each other all the *time* –

MIMI. You know, Greta – let me tell you something – let me tell you something, Greta –

GRETA. Does your man appreciate that? Or is this some kind of weird – believe me, I've seen all kinds of weird perverted shit from middle-aged people who you'd never imagine –

(slight pause)

MIMI. I'm not middle-aged.

GRETA. *(if she needs to believe that)* Okay.

MIMI. When you get to be my age, one thing I can promise you that you will not feel is middle-aged.

*(**GRETA** says nothing.)*

Jack is older than me, you know. He's quite a few years older. And anyway the point is that someday you will come to see that at a certain point in your life you come to value, to treasure, the people in your life and even when the relationship changes its nature you still want them in your life somehow. These people that have had this meaning in your life. These connections – you want to hold onto these rare and special connections in whatever form.

GRETA. That sounds like crap.

MIMI. And we don't call each other all the time. We're close. We speak. There's nothing wrong with that. You don't have any former boyfriends who you're still friends with?

GRETA. I could never just casually hang with someone I'd seen in the most intimate ways, stripped, raw, naked, fucking each other's brains out, humping and licking and sucking like beasts and knowing their secrets and their perversions and the way they smell, for him to know the way I smell, in the most intimate places, knowing every inch of each other and now we're just going to sit around and make polite *chit*-chat?

MIMI. Well everyone feels differently.

GRETA. I think that is fucking bizarre and hypocritical and only a person who can cut off part of themselves and live in denial, denial of intimacy, denial of the past – I could never do that.

MIMI. As I said, everyone's different.

GRETA. Your man doesn't mind?

MIMI. My "man" is not threatened, no.

GRETA. Do you buy that?

MIMI. He's stayed friends with a few ex-girlfriends and I don't mind. I don't mind at all, some of them I even like.

GRETA. He wants to fuck them.

MIMI. Listen Greta, you should go –

GRETA. Men always want that. Underneath. It's underneath everything.

MIMI. I think exes make wonderful friends – been there, done that, onward. I highly recommend it. In fact I wish I'd gone out with more people so I could have more former lovers now friends.

GRETA. In my opinion jealousy in a relationship is a sign of its strength, not its weakness.

MIMI. Okay. Greta. We could sit around debating this, but actually, I have to get to work. I've got what might be the only surviving letter from 12 years worth of intimate correspondence and that's really what I want to wrap my brain around right now, so you should talk to Jack about whatever it is you have to talk to him about. If things aren't working out in your relationship, it has absolutely nothing to do with me, I can promise you that.

GRETA. He told you that?

MIMI. What?

GRETA. That it isn't working out?

MIMI. You're *here*, aren't you?

GRETA. He visits you often, doesn't he.

MIMI. Greta…break-ups are painful things. I'm not trying to be patronizing. I went through some rough patches myself before Kai. Some really bad break-ups. And now I look back, and you know what? I'm grateful. Thank God. Thank God I got out. That's what you'll look back and think.

GRETA. I don't know why you keep insisting that we're breaking up. We've had some difficulties, okay, I'm sure he tells you that, I'm sure you know plenty of things about me that you shouldn't – same way I know things about you. Intimate things. But our sexual connection is better than ever, and to me that says a lot, that says the deepest thing.

MIMI. If you want my advice, Greta, which I'm quite sure that you don't, but since you came here, to my home, to my office, to my home office, I'm going to give it to you anyway – leave Jack. End it. Get on with your life.

GRETA. Why would you tell me that?

MIMI. Jack is a great guy, he's a wonderful friend, but he's a terrible boyfriend.

GRETA. You don't know what he's like now.

MIMI. Yes, I do.

GRETA. You don't know what he's like in a relationship. Unless you've been lying to me.

MIMI. I know – I know he's never going to be faithful to you. Okay? I'm sorry. He's not.

GRETA. Just because he wasn't faithful to you doesn't make him a faithless person.

(GRETA *stands to go.*)

I'm going to tell him I was here myself.

MIMI. That's up to you.

GRETA. I was thinking I wouldn't, but I'm an honest person. I'd ask you not to mention it, but I doubt you'd keep your word on that.

(*a pause*)

MIMI. Goodbye, Greta.

GRETA. *(cont.)* Sorry about finishing your orange juice.

MIMI. Not at all.

(**MIMI** *holds open the door as* **GRETA** *exits.* **MIMI** *pauses. After a moment* **MIMI** *picks up the phone to dial.*)

MIMI. *(into phone)* Hello? Are you there? It's Mimi. You have to call me. You have to call me right away – Jack.

End of Act I

ACT II

Scene One

(**MIMI** *pressed the buzzer as she studies a document. She goes to the coffee table, gets out a magnifying lens to get a better look. Knocking on the door. She's absorbed, doesn't notice at first. The doorbell, door knocking. She finally gets jarred from what's absorbing her and opens the door to* **JACK**.)

MIMI. Sorry.

JACK. I was out there for a while.

MIMI. Sorry, I spaced.

JACK. You buzzed me up –

MIMI. This Charles Dickens letter, this is a really good fake, I think.

JACK. Can you believe what's going on here?

MIMI. *(showing the page)* Look at this signature, you see – abrupt ending, too much ink, dead give-away. People don't end their own signatures so abruptly, you see?

JACK. Mimi – Mimi, that's fascinating, but I'm fucked here.

MIMI. Sorry. Right. Now what's happened? You said no one was hurt?

JACK. Not seriously. I'm totally fucked.

MIMI. The whole bar fell just fell?

JACK. It was the walls – their fucking walls. They had no insulation and then what happens is that they were basically rotting inside – from the moisture. Because of the heat in the kitchen. How am I supposed to know this, how they've built their walls? And in good faith I put up a beautiful slab of concrete and stone, now it falls, a woman breaks her foot or claims she did – am I to blame for that?

MIMI. It doesn't sound like you would be. I called Kai.

JACK. Thanks, Meems. What does he say?

MIMI. He's going to talk to another lawyer; he wants you to call him.

JACK. This bitch is going to name me in her suit.

MIMI. Don't you have insurance?

JACK. I'm not an architect. I'm not a contractor. I *trusted* them to build their walls *prop*erly, to build to code.

MIMI. Then I don't see why you'd be liable.

JACK. This lady broke her foot, or so she claims; she's probably going to claim she was an aspiring tap dancer, sue me for millions of dollars –

MIMI. It's not your fault.

JACK. I can't be responsible for other people's shoddy work.

(JACK *calms down. He sits on his chair.*)

I do like this chair.

(JACK *puts his head in his hands.*)

MIMI. Do you want something to eat? I'm starving.

(MIMI *goes to the kitchen.* JACK *speaks more loudly.*)

JACK. What have I *done*, that I am at the center of so much, so much *hostility*.

(MIMI *comes back with a bag of cookies.*)

Am I some kind of horrible person, that everyone is so angry with me?

MIMI. Phyllis seems happy with you.

JACK. I'm crazy about Phyllis. She's the one good thing right now. What does she say about me?

MIMI. She calls me all the time to tell me the fabulous things you say to her. She seems to believe everything you say.

JACK. What does that mean?

MIMI. Just that she believes you.

JACK. And you don't?

MIMI. That night with Greta phoning, it was a bit sticky – I wasn't sure Phyllis would stand for that.

JACK. Stand for what? It wasn't my fault.

MIMI. Jack, it's me, Mimi. I know you. I've known you for years.

JACK. What's the implication here?

MIMI. I know how you are. I know you're still sleeping with Greta. Or at least were. Or at least did that night.

JACK. It's not like that, Meems.

MIMI. Jack –

JACK. I'm not seeing Greta.

MIMI. And she really threatened suicide? That's why you were there?

JACK. Yes. She had. She's not stable.

MIMI. And you didn't do anything with her that night?

JACK. You sound like the D.A.

MIMI. She was here, Jack. She came to see me.

(*a pause*)

She didn't tell you? She said she was going to.

JACK. I've been a little busy. Jesus. Greta is absolutely out of her gourd. I cannot believe she came here. What did you say to her?

MIMI. I didn't say anything, Jack.

JACK. I'm not doing anything wrong.

(**MIMI** *stares at him; he sighs, caught out.*)

She's a sweet girl. She's depressed. I don't know what I'm doing.

MIMI. No, you don't, do you.

JACK. Why are you angry?

MIMI. Phyllis is my friend.

JACK. Mimi, I'm crazy about Phyllis. But I'm not married to her.

MIMI. You're making her a chair.

JACK. She loves my chairs.

MIMI. Why do you have to move so quickly?

JACK. She seems to be on the same schedule.

MIMI. You should tell her, at least.

JACK. Tell her what? That I'm a man? That when a beautiful girl takes off her clothes and sits on my lap and sticks her tits in my face I'm probably not going to be able to resist that?

MIMI. You know, Jack, you need help.

JACK. I take issue with that –

MIMI. You can't keep living this way.

JACK. – with that whole line of reasoning.

MIMI. All these women. All these messes. Aren't you sick of it yet?

JACK. This isn't *your* prerogative anymore.

MIMI. You're right. I don't care. It's fine. It's your life. You're right, I can't care anymore, how you choose to conduct your so-called love life. But Phyllis is my friend. And when I see you – when I see what you're doing. You're an addict, Jack.

JACK. This is what I hate.

MIMI. That I tell you the truth?

JACK. What is the truth, Mimi? I threaten the conventional choices you've made? "I'm an addict." What does that mean? Why does everyone have to pathologize sexuality that isn't their own? I've read all about the *puer aeternus*, okay? I'm probably better versed in all those therapeutic constructs than the rest of you. And I still know how to enjoy a good cigar.

MIMI. That's what's scary. You see it, you get it, but you won't change.

JACK. Why should I? I like women. I like fucking them. I don't make any pretenses otherwise.

MIMI. Then tell Phyllis you're still sleeping with Greta.

JACK. Why?

MIMI. If you think there's nothing wrong with it, maybe she'll agree. But doesn't she have a right to know what cards she's playing with?

(He looks at her.)

This is what makes you a liar, Jack.

JACK. Now you're on the "it's not that he did it, it's that he lied about doing it" committee? It's no one's business.

MIMI. She has a right to know.

JACK. I'm making her happy. You said so yourself.

MIMI. You, who always talks about integrity this and honesty that. You lie to women to get what you want. You lie to yourself, telling yourself what an honest, up-front, unhypocritical person you are. Okay, you're right, maybe Phyllis won't mind, maybe Phyllis wants to fuck around, too, but she should *know*.

JACK. I don't want to be with Greta.

*(**MIMI** stares him down.)*

If I'm still sleeping with Greta once in a while it is not a big deal. It doesn't affect what is going on between me and Phyllis. I never took a vow to anyone here.

MIMI. *(a joking tone)* The Jack dilemma: you want an interesting, independent woman, but an interesting, independent woman is never going to be able to put up with your shit.

JACK. Okay, thank you, Meems, appreciate the lecture from on high.

MIMI. Phyllis is great.

JACK. I agree.

MIMI. Don't screw it up with Phyllis.

JACK. I'm going back over to the restaurant.

MIMI. Kai said to tell you not to agree to anything until you meet with him.

JACK. Thanks, Meems. I'm sorry to unload on you.

MIMI. Rough day all around.

JACK. I'm not this evil person.

MIMI. I know that. I'm sorry, I ...I guess it's not my place to say.

*(**MIMI** stops herself from saying more. She and **JACK** look at each other for a beat; **MIMI** suddenly turns her gaze away, looking down. **JACK** looks down, as well. He sees the cassette tape he made; picks it up.)*

(recovering; brightly, and more distanced)

Oh, I told you we love the tape, didn't I? We listen to it all the time.

JACK. So you found a tape player?

*(**MIMI** is silent.)*

MIMI. We listen to it on the little thing.

JACK. *(teasing, but meaning it)* You're a liar, Mimi. You're a liar, too.

*(**JACK** hands **MIMI** the cassette tape as he goes. She is left alone, holding onto it.)*

Scene Two

(**PHYLLIS** *and* **MIMI** *are on the phone.*)

MIMI. Phyllis?

PHYLLIS. Mimi. There you are. I want to thank you.

MIMI. For what?

PHYLLIS. He's a real man. He's had a life.

MIMI. Phyllis, I –

PHYLLIS. He gets it. He gets me. Thank you. How can I thank you?

MIMI. I don't want to be thanked. For one thing, I really didn't do anything.

PHYLLIS. You're my "if not for." If not for you…

MIMI. I'd rather you not look at it that way.

PHYLLIS. At the very least I should thank you for breaking up with him.

MIMI. He pretty much broke up with me, Phil.

PHYLLIS. Funny how everything works out the way it's supposed to. I want to throw you a shower.

MIMI. Oh, God, Phil, no, I couldn't bear that.

PHYLLIS. It will be fun.

MIMI. Phyllis –
I don't want a shower. I don't want an engagement ring. I don't want to "register." I don't like all that – stuff.

PHYLLIS. God, when I get married, I'm going to do it up – I see a ten foot train, a veil, and a cake that goes through the roof.

MIMI. Whatever makes you happy.

PHYLLIS. Did I tell you he emails me five times a day? He's so smart. To have this intellectual connection – I've been, like, starving for that.

MIMI. I…hope it works out.

PHYLLIS. I know he's not a conventional guy, but I like that. The way he doesn't give a damn. I never would have expected it, but he's perfect for me, don't you think?

(after a pause) Mimi?

MIMI. I do know he's crazy about you.

PHYLLIS. Did he say that? What did he say?

MIMI. You know I hate being in the middle of this.

PHYLLIS. Can you imagine, me and Jack ending up together? How weird would that be?

MIMI. Pretty weird. Oh, hey, can you believe what time it is? I've gotta go.

Scene Three

(A bar. JACK and KAI each nurse drinks, go through legal papers.)

JACK. Thanks for helping me out.

KAI. No problem. Mimi asked me to, so...I need for you to explain a few points –

JACK. Lay it on me.

KAI. What's Visqueen?

JACK. That's a popular vapor barrier.

KAI. Which is?

JACK. You want that on the warm side of a wall to prevent air from migrating through to the cool side and condensing.

KAI. Otherwise? I'm sure we studied this in high school, but I've cleared out those brain cells.

JACK. See, buildings used to be more loosely built. Masonry, that allows for air flow. Now air migrates through the wall, gets trapped in there and reaches its dew point *inside* the wall. This causes rot. So we need to create moisture and vapor barriers to stop the transpiration of warm moist air. You follow?

KAI. Otherwise air turns to moisture right inside the wall.

JACK. You could say that, yes. If it reaches its dew point – the temperature and pressure at which vapor condenses into liquid. You know, like on this glass.

(holding up his glass)

The moisture in the air is coming into contact with this cold glass and condensing. Warmer air can hold more moisture, and then when you introduce a cold surface, wham, when the air hits a certain temperature against the glass, the vapor condenses to water.

KAI. That's how we get dew?

JACK. When the air warms up more quickly than the earth, right. You see they had that kitchen, all the heat-generating equipment in that kitchen, right up against the refrigerated side of the bar, with no insulation in between.

KAI. And you didn't check this –

JACK. I wouldn't. I was brought in to do a very specific task. I happen to know about this stuff, but I don't need to.

KAI. Right. I am surprised you don't carry insurance.

JACK. I design furniture. I don't build buildings. The contractor is the one who oversees all this. I don't think that woman really broke her foot.

KAI. Probably looking for a settlement.

JACK. I don't think I personally should have to pay anything.

KAI. We should be able to get you out of this. It's not my area, but I have a colleague – I'll put you in touch with the right person.

JACK. I want to pay for all this, of course. For your time, too.

KAI. That won't be necessary.

JACK. At least let me buy the drinks.

*(**KAI** shrugs "okay"; off his glass:)*

KAI. I don't think I've ever much thought about where the moisture on a glass comes from. In the air all the time, all the time; that's interesting.

JACK. Everything is volatile.

KAI. It seems so.

JACK. Certain triggers – certain triggers and environmental conditions, they make visible, make manifest what's already there. Take that waitress – that is a gorgeous woman, is she not?

KAI. I'd have to agree with you there.

JACK. And maybe I'm in a relationship, and maybe I think it's a good, stable thing, but then there is the introduction of this other being, and a once stable thing is rendered unstable. A question mark of possibility arises.

KAI. How's it going with Phyllis, Jack?

JACK. Phyllis is great. Phyllis is a phenomenal person.

KAI. I've always liked her very much.

JACK. But already, already I'm constantly defending myself. This bubble of suspicion I'm under – does Mimi question everything you do?

KAI. I try not to give her cause.

JACK. A relationship should not be mutual self-defense. And Phil, Phil can't admit to herself that the reason she's stayed single so long is because she's really much happier on her own.

KAI. I don't get that impression.

JACK. I think she's afraid of making the sacrifices, the compromises it takes. If she would admit that to herself, she'd be a much happier person.

KAI. Maybe she just hasn't met her match yet.

JACK. I'm not saying it can't work out with us. It can. It might. I hope it will. I really like her enormously.

KAI. Then *make* it work out, Jack. It may well be within your power to do so.

JACK. Now I'm looking at our waitress friend over there, I'm watching this other person, this stranger, and I want to know what her tits look like. I just want to know. Is that wrong?

KAI. I used to be like that. Undressed almost every women I saw – what would it be like – imagined that –

JACK. What happened?

KAI. I turned 16.

JACK. It's not just sexual. It may start there, but it's – it's wanting to commune with another soul, to connect, to know this person wholly, totally – Am I supposed to cut that off?

KAI. Not every itch has to be scratched, in my opinion. The feeling will pass. That urgency.

JACK. Half the people I know, men and women – and I'm not including you, Kai, but half of them, make that most of them, they're the walking dead. I won't become that. I don't think it's a natural thing, to be with one person for the rest of one's life – in the interest of what, safety? I don't believe in playing it safe. There's a biological reality we're fighting against.

KAI. And there's evolution.

JACK. Evolution?

KAI. I'd like to advance beyond my biological reality. Because you're right, there's fear – cutting ourselves off out of fear, out of conventionality – but if you want to talk about knowing a person wholly, totally – is that really what you're doing? There will always be more women, women who are interesting, and beautiful, and fascinating, and I won't get to be with all of them, but I will get further – and deeper – with the one beautiful and interesting and fascinating woman I've chosen. And I wouldn't do anything to hurt her. It's that simple.

JACK. Nice wedding toast, but you really think that's enough insulation?

KAI. Insulation?

JACK. You think that's enough insulation to keep those feelings contained? In the long run? When you're a little bored, and a little pissed off, let's say, and you miss certain feelings, and you think you might be able to get away with it…

KAI. If I knew I'd get away with shop lifting, I still wouldn't do it. Not to sound goody goody.

JACK. How about a hit of heroin? Guaranteed, absolute bliss, one time only, no consequences, guaranteed no consequences, would you try it?

KAI. It doesn't work that way, "no consequences." There's always a cost.

JACK. "Always a cost." I hate that way of thinking; okay then, there's also a cost to being bourgeois, conventional, complacent and comfortable.

KAI. You know what? I don't need to defend my desire for monogamy.

JACK. I'm sorry, I'm not trying to threaten you.

KAI. You're not. You know, Jack, I've been a newness junkie, too. I know what that's about. But even newness gets old after a while.

(**JACK** *pauses, takes a sip of his drink.*)

JACK. I like you, Kai.

> *(another beat)*

I'm happy as shit for Mimi.

> (**KAI** *pauses, sipping his drink.*)

KAI. I don't think of shit as happy.

> *(another beat)*

JACK. That's funny.

KAI. *(of papers)* Tell you what, I'll look these over. Connect you with the right person.

JACK. I'm grateful.

KAI. I'll call you if I have any more questions, but I'm hopeful we can make this go away.

JACK. That's great, Kai, I'm really – thanks. You know I want us to be friends. I'd love it if we could all be friends. Mimi's family to me. So I think of you – I'd like to think of you – at the very least as someone who doesn't actively dislike me.

KAI. I don't dislike you, Jack.

JACK. Then good.

KAI. I'd even go so far as to say I like you. Any resentment I have is not because of the current dynamic, but because you hurt Mimi. You cheated on her, and you lied to her, and you hurt her. And that angers me, it does, because I really can't stand thinking of Mimi getting hurt.

JACK. I understand. We hurt each other, in truth, but look, I understand.

KAI. *(taking out his wallet)* Check in with me tomorrow, we'll see where we are.

> (**KAI** *tries to put money on the table.* **JACK** *stops him.*)

JACK. One more round?

KAI. I'm afraid not.

JACK. The wife to get home to.

KAI. That's right.

JACK. I say that with admiration.

KAI. Thanks for the drink, Jack. And the chair. Have I properly thanked you for the chair yet? We like our chair.

JACK. I'm glad you like it. Do you really? Because understanding what goes into a chair...that's a huge enterprise, if you can believe. People have spent years, years of their lives on a single chair. Maybe that sounds silly to you, but I think it's quite moving, to think about the body, to think about gravity and structure and stability and rest – I'm really just at the beginning of understanding what makes a good chair.

KAI. I think you've done very well.

(KAI *pats* JACK*'s back, starts to go.*)

JACK. There's this amazing chair – this guy Pesce, totally brilliant, he did this chair – late sixties, '68 I think – it's a round, red – obscenely red, soft, pliable, wide, badass chair. He modeled it on the Venus of Wilhendorf.

KAI. What's that?

JACK. I'm sure you've seen the image somewhere – classic fertility goddess. And you're meant to sink into this chair, this chair that's abstracted from the shape of a woman in an exaggerated cartoon way, and the footstool's this big red sphere tied to the leg like a ball and chain. Pesce says he saw a woman as a prisoner of herself against her will, and he wanted to convey that.

(KAI *nods, standing, his coat in hand.*)

(*lost for a moment, facing out*) But I've sat in that chair, I've been engulfed by the Venus, and I felt quite sure that it was the other way around, that the prisoner was me.

KAI. A prisoner of the woman, or a prisoner of you own nature?

JACK. I'll have to think about that. I will think about that.

(KAI *goes, leaving* JACK *alone at the bar.*)

Scene Four

(MIMI and KAI's apartment. They sit on couch eating Chinese take-out.)

KAI. What I think is interesting...

MIMI. Yes?

KAI. Very interesting.

MIMI. Will you please finish your sentence already?

KAI. I'm eating.

MIMI. That is so male. You start a sentence like it's a carrot – here's a really fabulous thing I'm going to say – and then you make me wait. You love that, don't you.

KAI. I love my General Tso's chicken.

MIMI. Will you please tell me what is interesting all ready? Making me beg for what you already have dangled – that's what you're doing, you know.

KAI. Excuse me, I was swallowing. What's interesting to me is that you tell Jack, you warn Jack, but you don't say a word to Phyllis.

MIMI. What could I possibly say to her? And if they work it out, if they manage somehow to work it out, then I'd always be the asshole who tried to interfere.

KAI. You're so invested in protecting Jack.

MIMI. I thought I was protecting Phyllis. I don't want to hurt her. If she knew about Greta – she'd, I don't know, I couldn't do that to her.

KAI. You're not doing it to her; Jack is.

MIMI. If Phyllis really wanted to know about Greta, she'd have figured it out already. She'd have figured it out that night Greta called, don't you think?

KAI. I think you've suddenly changed your entire philosophy. What happened to "a person has a right to know"?

MIMI. But I know how these things go. If I say something now, she'll only be angry with me. Kill the messenger and all that.

KAI. That sounds like a good way to let yourself off the hook. And now you want me to help him get off the hook, too.

MIMI. That's different. He's being sued unfairly.

KAI. Okay. But maybe you should retire the matchmaking shingle. How's it going with Dickens?

MIMI. I'm immersed in other people's lives, aren't I.

KAI. Tell me, Meem – is it a forgery or the real thing?

MIMI. You're just going to change the subject so easily?

KAI. Yes.

MIMI. I can't authenticate it. It was written to his supposed mistress, I told you that, right?

KAI. Ellen Ternan. So it's a fake?

MIMI. It's strange – the ink tests out, and the paper, no anachronistic terminology in the text – but then there's this signature: it's a little too legible, and these blunt starts and endings – there should be a continuing stroke. Dickens tended to sign off with a flourish, even in a love letter.

KAI. More so in a love letter, I'd think.

> **MIMI.** So all I can think is, it must have been forged while he was alive. Do you get what this might mean? (**KAI** *enters.* **MIMI** *looks up from her desk, excited.*)

KAI. Blackmail?

MIMI. Exactly. Someone must have been trying to blackmail Charles Dickens – and, and maybe they even succeeded – that's what this letter is. He had such a prim and proper reputation, he couldn't risk losing his readership.

KAI. And who would want to blackmail Charles Dickens?

MIMI. I don't know; who wouldn't want to? He was famous, he was rich, he'd pretty much abandoned his wife and kids – see, of course he did really have a mistress.

KAI. Of course.

MIMI. But he was too smart and too discreet to leave evidence. Why did you say "of course"?

KAI. What?

MIMI. Like what, like all great men have mistresses?

KAI. Probably back then, when the wife was taking care of ten kids and opportunity presented itself – and not just "great" men, though that would certainly up the opportunity quotient.

MIMI. That's a fucked thing to think.

KAI. To "think"? Are you censoring my mind?

MIMI. But I can't believe you think that way.

KAI. Mimi, don't go where you're going. I do not want to cheat on you.

MIMI. Right now. Right now, okay, but what will stop you? What will eventually stop you?

KAI. A, you won't have *ten* kids, B, I won't be so great?

MIMI. It's not a joke, Kai.

KAI. I can't take you seriously right now. I have to justify myself to your ex-boyfriend, and now to you?

(a pause)

This is not about us, or me. You've let his ideas seep into our life.

MIMI. You can ask me to stop being friends with him.

KAI. I don't want to ask you that. We're not in junior high school. Do you want me to ask you that?

MIMI. No, I –

KAI. I don't accept the alpha chimp cliché.

MIMI. The what cliché?

KAI. I'm supposed to get angry. I'm supposed to make demands. To show my love for you by making jealous demands. If I'm too understanding, that's a weakness. I don't accept that. I won't let you turn me into the type of person I'm not. If I'm made to feel distrustful, jealous, on the look-out, well, I won't be sneaking around reading your journals, looking at your receipts, cracking your email code. I won't demean myself. I will leave first. Do you understand? If I'm made to feel that way, like a spy in my own home, I will leave.

MIMI. I know that about you.

KAI. And if I made you feel that way…I would be miserable to make you feel that way. So if it's what you want – to be kept on your toes like that, to worry just enough to get your blood pumping – I'm not going to provide that service.

(*KAI starts to go.*)

MIMI. I don't want you to. Where are you going?

KAI. He's not every man. He's not me. You let him seep in…his ideas…but he has nothing to do with us.

MIMI. I know that.

(*KAI turns back. He goes closer to* **MIMI**.)

KAI. We should have a real wedding.

MIMI. We hate weddings.

KAI. Maybe there is something to getting up in front of people. In front of our family, our friends.

MIMI. We bonded over how we both hate the whole wedding thing on our first date.

KAI. Maybe we don't need to dismiss a centuries-old ritual.

MIMI. This is how it starts, isn't it.

(*MIMI sits in* **JACK**'s *chair, oblivious to where she is sitting.*)

This is how we begin to shrink-wrap our lives, sealed in plastic, airless – we shut ourselves down a little more all the time, just because we're afraid.

KAI. I wasn't marrying you out of fear, Mimi. But I'm sorry that's what it's about for you.

(*KAI exits.* **MIMI** *stands and starts after him.*)

MIMI. You're going? You're just going to go?

(*KAI closes the door behind him.* **MIMI** *stays still.*)

Scene Five

(MIMI and KAI's apartment, the next day. PHYLLIS enters with a small grocery bag.)

PHYLLIS. This was outside your door.

MIMI. Thanks.

(MIMI takes a carton of orange juice out of the bag.)

Oh.

PHYLLIS. Somebody dropped off orange juice?

MIMI. Apparently.

PHYLLIS. Are you sick?

MIMI. No.

PHYLLIS. Did you leave it there for a reason?

MIMI. No.

PHYLLIS. Then you probably shouldn't drink it.

MIMI. No.

PHYLLIS. I'm angry at you.

MIMI. Everyone is.

PHYLLIS. He's still sleeping with Greta.

MIMI. I suspected.

PHYLLIS. And God knows who else. What do you mean you suspected?

MIMI. I'm sorry.

PHYLLIS. You knew.

MIMI. I wasn't sure. I'm going to fix us a drink.

(MIMI takes the orange juice carton and goes to the kitchen. PHYLLIS looks at the chair. She takes out her cell phone and speed dials.)

PHYLLIS. *(into phone)* Hi, Phyllis again. The furniture I told you about? That isn't going to work out for the shoot. Sorry, but I can't pin the designer down, he's a bit of a flake. Wanted to give you the heads up on that.

(She makes another call.)

PHYLLIS. *(into phone)* And another thing, Jack, I won't be needing your furniture for the shoot. The magazine changed its mind. Fuck off.

(She clicks off, satisfied with herself. MIMI *comes back carrying a pitcher and glasses.)*

MIMI. This is a kier. Sort of. I used a cherry-flavored thing instead of framboise.

PHYLLIS. And you didn't warn me. That's what I can't understand.

MIMI. Try it. I've been making them – I hardly ever drink but I had this bottle from a Christmas basket last year – who sends that stuff?

PHYLLIS. Because really I feel like, like you set me up with a devil. Really. With someone evil. And what I want to know is, did you, did you intend to hurt me? Did you intend to see me get hurt and was there some, maybe not conscious but some underlying desire to, to punish me by sicking this, this really bad guy onto me, onto my heart? This is a Shirley Temple.

MIMI. It's good, isn't it?

PHYLLIS. It's cough medicine. Jesus, Mimi, what did you put in this, Robutussin?

MIMI. What I thought is, it might work out; how can I say it won't? And I thought: quite possibly he's changed; he may well have changed. You seemed to really like him so I thought, who am I to spoil that? Do I spoil that? I mean what happened with us, it was so long ago.

PHYLLIS. People don't change. Please.

MIMI. I hate to think that.

PHYLLIS. Think it. Men especially don't change.

MIMI. Well I like to think it's always possible.

PHYLLIS. I don't even believe that you believe that it is. Would your experience bear out thinking that I don't think so.

MIMI. I'd like to think that I can change. That people can.

PHYLLIS. He hit on my photographer. I introduced him to people, people for the shoot, he hit on one of my female photographers who is not even cute, who is like a homely pig, I'm telling you, and he hit on the, like, sub-makeup artist, this grungy little peon.

MIMI. Phyllis…

PHYLLIS. Do you realize how humiliating that is? I have news for you, he is fucking out of control. He is a fucking out of control fucker. I have news for you.

MIMI. I don't think…he's as bad as…that bad.

PHYLLIS. He's your friend. I took that as a testament to his character; that you would be his friend.

MIMI. He's on his way over here.

PHYLLIS. What?

MIMI. He wants another chance. He wants to see you.

PHYLLIS. How could you –

MIMI. He wants to talk with you, Phyllis.

PHYLLIS. That is so –

MIMI. He's crazy about you.

PHYLLIS. You're demented.

MIMI. I do think he does love you.

PHYLLIS. And you –

MIMI. I'm sorry. I wasn't up for thwarting his plans right now.

PHYLLIS. Jesus, Mimi.

MIMI. He asked me to put in a word and I said I would.

PHYLLIS. You know what I think is the sickest thing of all? Not him – not his behavior – but yours. This is a man who decimates women. Who annihilates them. Who is an absolute liar and who trashes one woman after another with his lies. He draws them in, seduces, pulls the rug out from under. He does this on a regular basis and you condone it.

MIMI. I condone it?

PHYLLIS. You don't condemn it.

MIMI. Of course I do. I find it abhorrent, that aspect –

PHYLLIS. That "aspect"? It's who he is.

MIMI. It's not all of who he is.

PHYLLIS. Would you be friends with a racist? How about a Nazi? A charming little Jew-hater from the S.S.? I don't think so. But women, if the victim is women…

(downing the rest of the drink)

You hide under your convenient little "I won't judge another" mantra and then you push him onto a friend, you encourage it, even now you sit there arranging a way for him to continue…you're his goddam pimp.

(MIMI *is silent for a moment.)*

MIMI. I could have handled things better.

PHYLLIS. How about a wonderful, lovely, smart, funny, fabulously engaging man who just happens to have this one little thing – his predilection for raping kindergartners?

MIMI. I think that's extreme.

PHYLLIS. I think he's extreme. I think excusing his behavior is extreme. Great guy, happens to drive women to the brink of suicide.

MIMI. I did in fact think that there was a chance – he's convincing, he's very convincing, and he managed to convince me that – somehow…

(MIMI *shakes her head, at a loss.)*

PHYLLIS. I'm sure you'll figure out a rationalization. He fucked you over, what is it, your goal to see to it that someone else gets fucked over, too?

MIMI. So why would you go out with someone who "fucked me over," your words?

PHYLLIS. There you go.

MIMI. I'm sorry, but you liked him all on your own, don't blame me. I hate to remind you but you overlooked quite a lot yourself, because you liked him a lot, a whole lot. I didn't think it was my place – *given* my history with him, which you knew well enough – in fact I thought it would be highly suspect if I tried to stand between – and as a matter of fact I don't believe you would have listened to me. You were thrilled he was interested. You were thrilled. And I don't think anything I could have said at that point would have made you give him up.

PHYLLIS. You see? I knew you would come up with something. You can rationalize it all very nicely if you choose. How easy. How simple for you. It must be lovely to have a brain so well programmed to block out anything that doesn't fit into your good opinion of yourself.

(PHYLLIS *starts for the door. She opens the door.* MIMI *stops her.*)

MIMI. You knew our history. You knew we'd lived together for two years, you knew he broke my heart at the time. And you went out with him anyway. Some people would say *that's* crossing a line.

PHYLLIS. But you encouraged – you even suggested –

MIMI. I never suggested. You wanted to go out with him, and what the hell was I supposed to say? How selfish would that be, hey, "I'm getting married but you better stay away from my old boyfriends, I have dibs on them"? I was trying to be a grown-up about it.

(GRETA *comes to the door. They don't see her at first.*)

But then you, you gloated about how Jack was declaring true love like he'd never felt for *anyone* before, dedicating chairs to you – you wanted to show me that he loved you more than me.

PHYLLIS. (*quietly*) That's not true. I didn't think you cared; that's not true.

MIMI. You wanted to win.

PHYLLIS. Sorry, hon, but that is your issue; Jack is no prize as far as I'm concerned.

(PHYLLIS *and* MIMI *both suddenly see* GRETA *in the doorway.* GRETA *steps inside.*)

GRETA. Did you get the orange juice? I left it here earlier; I felt bad taking your last glass. It's so weird, I come here and I immediately crave orange juice. I develop this overpowering thirst.

(*extending hand to* **PHYLLIS**)

Hi, I'm Greta.

PHYLLIS. Oh, right, the aspiring actress slash dancer slash wrist-slasher.

(**MIMI** *holds out a glass.*)

MIMI. Have a drink, Greta.

GRETA. I don't drink alcohol.

MIMI. I'll have another.

MIMI. (*to* **PHYLLIS,** *off her look*) I should have told you. She came here. She was upset. She thought *we* were sleeping together. Me and Jack. I should have told you she was here, but I wasn't sure what good it would do. I didn't think it was my place. I didn't – I just didn't think it was my place.

PHYLLIS. Your "place"? You were worried about your "place"?

GRETA. You set up my boyfriend?

MIMI. No, I – I –

PHYLLIS. Always so concerned about what is appropriate, about not stepping out of bounds – well humility is a form of cruelty when it's an excuse to put yourself, your ideals about yourself first. Your "place" – you set us up, for Christ's sake.

MIMI. (*to* **GRETA**) And he said it was over between you two. He had moved on. He was looking to meet someone new.

PHYLLIS. Hence you sicked him on me.

GRETA. I'm willing to fight for him.

PHYLLIS. That's lovely, dear…but I really don't want him.

(*leaving; to* **MIMI**)

Tell Jack hello. It's a shame you two can't get back together; you might consider it, you seem to be very well-matched.

(**PHYLLIS** *goes.*)

GRETA. You should have told me about her.

MIMI. I think you should leave, Greta.

GRETA. I thought your generation believed in female solidarity.

MIMI. I need to be alone right now.

GRETA. I know he's coming here. I need to talk to him.

MIMI. Can't you do it someplace else?

GRETA. I'd rather confront him on neutral territory.

MIMI. This is not neutral territory. This is my home.

GRETA. Your home and your office.

MIMI. I don't work anymore anyway, haven't you noticed? My friend – that was my – friend.

GRETA. What do you do again? Sell old papers?

MIMI. That's right. Create value where there is none – manipulate desire.

(**MIMI** *closes her eyes and presses her hands against her face.*)

My friend...I thought...my friend.

(**GRETA** *begins to shake out her limbs, as if at the beginning of a dance.*)   .

GRETA. I know Jack's a fucker sometimes. But he's afraid. It was getting too real with us, and he got afraid. We store fear in our bodies, we store the fear and the hurt, and there are acupressure points for that.

(**GRETA** *goes through a series of dance postures, starting with a relaxed, graceful stretch and becoming increasingly aggressive and agitated.* **MIMI** *opens her eyes slowly.*)

GRETA. *(cont.)* I love him with everything I've got, how many people get to love that way? I see the fear and the hurt places and I have a lot of compassion in my heart for him because my background, it was not what you would call in any way "positive." Jack and I share that. We're soul mates, me and Jack. You don't give that up just because a guy puts his dick in the wrong place when he starts to freak.

(**GRETA** *ends her routine with a kick and jab in* **MIMI***'s direction.* **MIMI** *opens her eyes.*)

MIMI. *(quietly)* I'd really rather stay out of it if you don't mind.

GRETA. I know I'm a confrontational person. I'm a dancer. I have to confront stuff all the time. Pain. My own limitations. The music. I have this relationship to music where I kind of, like, confront it.

(**GRETA** *offers up another jabbing dance gesture.*)

MIMI. *(still quietly, shaken)* You should go, Greta. I don't think he's going to come after all so, so I think it would be best for you to go.

(**GRETA** *starts to go.*)

GRETA. I don't mind a good struggle. Maybe that's why I really don't mind Jack. Why I really believe it will work out, until it isn't meant to work out anymore, but I just don't believe Jack and I are at the end of what we have to work out together and learn from each other yet.

(**MIMI** *suddenly goes to look for a document; rifles through papers urgently.* **GRETA** *exits.* **MIMI** *continues to rifle through papers until she finds the document she's been looking for. She holds onto it, studying it closely, hands beginning to shake, as lights shift…*)

(*Eight years earlier.* **JACK** *enters.* **MIMI** *holds out a letter. Her hands are shaking.*)

MIMI. What is this?

JACK. Where did you get that?

MIMI. What is this, Jack?

JACK. Don't go through my mail.

MIMI. What the *fuck*.

JACK. She has an active imagination.

MIMI. *(reading from letter)* "I long to feel you inside me again."

JACK. It's what she wants.

MIMI. Explain the "again."

JACK. She's crazy. She imagines –

MIMI. No, Jack, you're crazy. You're fucking crazy. And I'm an insane person for having believed you. Why is it, Jack, that all these women get so obsessed with you? You think you're such a god?

JACK. Well...

MIMI. You put it out there. You fucking dangle it. Your fucking cock. You're a sick bastard.

JACK. It's not working between us. It's obvious that you hate me.

MIMI. I hate you? I hate you? I hate you because you are a fucking pig! How many women, Jack? How many women have you fucked under my nose?

JACK. You're going to have to calm down.

MIMI. I don't want to calm down. You're a sick fucking piece of shit bastard.

JACK. Listen to yourself.

MIMI. You turned me into this. You've fucking turned me into this!

JACK. Mimi, sit down. I'm going to get you a glass of water.

MIMI. You liar. You fucking liar. Why did you do this? Is it a fucking game to you? You beg me to move in with you, beg me to live here when I didn't even want to, I wanted to wait but you push and you push and you wear me down so that what, so you can fuck every fat bitch whore like Lisa who comes your way right under my nose?

JACK. I did not do anything with Lisa.

MIMI. Liar.

JACK. I'm not going to do this.

MIMI. Who else, you fuck? Annie? Stephanie? Nicole? You did, didn't you, that night you went to dinner with Nicole, a five hour dinner in a restaurant, it's fucking impossible to spend five hours at a Chinese restaurant. You're a walking fucking disease, you've put me at risk, at risk of dying, you fucking sick, sick fuck.

(He starts to go.)

Where are you going?

JACK. I'm not going to sit around and listen to this.

MIMI. You're not going to leave me.

JACK. Why would you want to stay with a "sick, sick fuck"?

MIMI. This is what you've done to me. This is what you've turned me into. I'm reduced. Fucking reduced. I trusted you. I trusted people. I believed in people. This is what you've destroyed. Now I go digging around in your things like an animal, like a fucking sad pathetic rodent going through your garbage, your fucking garbage you're a soul killer, that's what you are a soul killer.

*(**JACK** tries to touch her.)*

Go, you fuck. Just go. Go destroy somebody else you fucking monster.

*(**JACK** goes. Light change. The buzzer is buzzing. More insistently now. **MIMI** presses it. She calms herself, opens the door to **JACK**.)*

JACK. What took you so long?

MIMI. I was indisposed.

JACK. "Indisposed"? You can tell me you were on the pot, Meems. Phyllis isn't here?

MIMI. No.

JACK. Are you all right?

MIMI. Fine.

*(**JACK** pours the orange juice into a mug on the table, hands it to her.)*

JACK. Here.

MIMI. Thanks.

JACK. Can I open a bottle?

MIMI. Sure.

JACK. Oh, I got you and Kai –

(He takes out two tiny speakers.)

JACK. They're actually pretty great speakers. Beautifully designed. They may even make your little Walkman sound half-decent. And there are two of them.

(MIMI *takes the speakers.*)

I would have got you guys a boom box but I love these little guys.

(JACK *goes into the kitchen.* MIMI *looks at the speakers. She sets them down.*)

JACK. *(O.S.)* I'm going to open the white, okay? God, what a crazy day. I think I have another restaurant commission, so I guess –

(as he enters with a wine bottle and three glasses)

So I guess the Tapas place isn't being held against me. Which, even that, they've apologized profusely and asked me to re-build. Which I don't think I will, but I guess they've managed to settle with the lady quickly. Thank God she wasn't one of those complete wackos who want a million dollars for drinking coffee that's too hot and dribbling a bit on their chins. Oh, should I not bring out a glass for Phyllis? I shouldn't. I should be surprised by her arrival.

MIMI. She left.

JACK. What?

MIMI. She was here, she left.

JACK. I'm that late?

MIMI. She didn't want to see you.

JACK. You told her I was coming?

MIMI. Yes, I did.

JACK. I thought the point was to not tell her I was coming.

MIMI. To ambush her, right.

JACK. That was our plan.

MIMI. Plan of attack failed to hit desired target. Mission not accomplished.

JACK. I take it she's still angry.

MIMI. I'd cross the Phyllis possibility off your list, Jack. Phyllis is not in a forgiving mood.

JACK. She got you angry at me, too.

MIMI. Not angry. I got yelled at myself.

JACK. And now you're taking her side.

MIMI. It's not about sides.

JACK. I didn't do anything wrong.

MIMI. You fucked around on her. A lot of people don't appreciate that.

JACK. We were just starting.

MIMI. Not a good way to start.

JACK. We should begin at 100% commitment, take vows before we even really know each other? Who knew where it was going to go…

MIMI. Well she felt misled.

JACK. Don't look at me like I'm some kind of deviant.

MIMI. Greta came by.

JACK. Greta again? Are you kidding me?

MIMI. You missed a lovely little party.

JACK. She's psycho.

MIMI. And that's why you're still sleeping with her?

JACK. *(a beat; trying to make light)* You know I find "psycho" a very appealing quality in a woman.

MIMI. I'm not laughing.

JACK. What do you want me to say? Greta is a good kid. She wants me. She's nice to me. That's a nice change, being with someone who's nice to me.

MIMI. So go be with Greta. She probably is right for you, Jack; she knows about Phyllis, and God knows who else, and she's willing to stick it out anyway. That could be a quality that works for you – someone who's willing to take all your crap.

JACK. What is the problem here?

MIMI. Why are we friends, Jack?

JACK. You need reminding? I'm charming, loyal, brilliant…

MIMI. When you think about it, I'm surprised we're still friends.

(a pause)

JACK. We're more than friends, ⌐
    other – even when we hate e⌐
    And life is really, really, really ⌐

MIMI. I'd forgotten how angry I was ⌐
    ing, looking back, that I got past ⌐

JACK. Basically I let you scream your ⌐
    phone calling me regularly to tell m⌐
    and I pretty much took it until you'd ⌐ of
    your system. Plus you met Kai.

MIMI. We were friends again before I met Kai.

JACK. The truth is you were glad to get rid of me. I think
    you knew in your heart that you didn't want me, that
    we weren't right for each other, and that probably
    allowed you to see that it wasn't entirely my fault.

MIMI. That's convenient.

JACK. What is all this renewed hostility?

    (pause)

MIMI. I think you should bear some of the responsibility.
    For the fall. I think when you put up a 200-pound
    piece of concrete and stone it's your responsibility to
    ensure that the method of support is sound. It's your
    responsibility to make sure that the walls aren't rotting
    inside.

JACK. Okay, Meems.

MIMI. There are consequences. There have to be conse-
    quences.

JACK. No one's denying that.

MIMI. I lived with you in a state of constant insecurity. It
    didn't start that way. I was not, previously, a jealous or
    snooping person. Do you know what it's like to live
    with someone making secret, sneaking glances above
    your head with waitresses, with store clerks, with your
    best friends? No one is off limits with you. If you want
    it, you make a grab for it, and if it causes a shitload of
    pain, of grief, of absolute devastation, you don't care;
    you won't be denied. Of course it took me a long time

believe anything was really happening; I couldn't
believe it; I needed evidence, a cold hard authentic
document that couldn't be denied but even then you
tried to wriggle your way out.

JACK. And ten years later you think we haven't gone over
this territory?

MIMI. I need to go over it again.

JACK. This is because you think I wasn't good to Phyllis?
You think I screwed over your friend?

MIMI. I know you screwed her over.

JACK. Look, don't set me up with your friends anymore.
Okay? But I'll tell you something – if she wanted a conventional, bourgeois, aspiring husband, it's pretty clear
she should have looked elsewhere; the fact is your
friend Phyllis hates herself for not wanting what she
thinks she is supposed to want and hates every man for
not fixing her life for her.

MIMI. Have you ever noticed that you are so good at the
insta-analyses for everyone but yourself?

JACK. Mimi, if you had the choice you'd be just like me.

MIMI. What the hell does that mean?

JACK. You've bought into it. I respect that, that's your deci-
sion, but are you telling me you wouldn't want to feel
it ever again? The newness, the excitement, the first
kiss, the first touch, the falling into someone else? You
don't want that ever, ever, ever again? And now you
have to condemn me because I'm not willing to give it
up. As such I'm a threat. I'm here to remind you that
biology had something else in mind.

MIMI. *(matter-of-fact)* Take your chair back.

JACK. What?

MIMI. *(evenly)* Take it back. Take it out of here. Get it out
of our lives.

*(She picks up the chair and place it in his arms. He
stands there holding it. She goes back to her desk, upset,
not wanting to look at him. He puts down chair and
goes to her. She moves papers around –)*

JACK. Meems, we're family, you and I – Meems…

MIMI. I'm blowing it. Maybe I've already blown it.

(A piece of the paper she's holding, brittle, cracks off.)

(overly emotional) Shit. This survived for 150 years before I got my hands on it. What the hell is wrong with me?

(beaking down; to herself)

Dammit, am I just one of those people who needs to be kept ever so slightly unsafe in order to feel… desire?

(A pause. JACK *goes to her; puts a hand on her shoulder to comfort her, though he is tentative, not overly affectionate; there is physical distance between them.)*

JACK. If that's your worry, rest assured, no one is completely safe.

*(*MIMI, *without looking up but with tenderness:)*

MIMI. I need for you to go, Jack.

JACK. If I were you…

(He stops, changing direction, to himself now.)

…if I were you, I'd probably …tell me to go.

*(*MIMI *smiles, just slightly, quietly. A pause between them. She looks at him now.)*

MIMI. I have to let you go.

*(*JACK *looks at her. A sort of nod between them. He goes to his chair.)*

JACK. Meanwhile I'm going to have a fucking good time…

(hoisting the chair over his shoulder)

…and I'm going to make some fucking beautiful chairs.

*(*JACK *goes, taking the chair with him.* MIMI *watches him go.)*

Scene Six

*(**MIMI** sits alone with a document – the one that cracked. She is repairing it carefully. **KAI** enters. He watches her for a moment, goes to her.)*

KAI. I went down to City Hall this morning. There were all these brides dressed in white...even though they were just going to go into this room to get some papers signed they were all dressed up. It's like another country down there...and there's this air of excitement – of things just starting out.

(taking a plastic bouquet of roses from his briefcase)

There were these vendors selling plastic bouquets in the plaza; bouquets and hot dogs from the same cart.

*(**KAI** hands **MIMI** the bouquet of flowers.)*

MIMI. Roses. Nice. Plastic lasts forever, anyway.

KAI. I'm sure we could destroy it if we tried.

MIMI. I particularly like the gobs of glue all over the petals.

KAI. I think those are supposed to be dew drops, Mimi.

*(**MIMI** stares at the bouquet for a moment.)*

MIMI. Oh. Right. Drops of morning dew.

KAI. I lied when I said I wouldn't get jealous; wouldn't stand for that. I've been seething, really.

MIMI. *(looking up at **KAI**)* Why do I have to be afraid I've lost something in order to find out how I really feel? How much I...

(She tears up; hard to continue.)

KAI. Desire creates value? Something like that?

MIMI. I have all these documents here at home, and I don't think I'm taking care of them properly...I'm afraid they're not going to last, Kai.

KAI. We need to protect them better, that's all.

*(**MIMI** shows **KAI** the document she was repairing:)*

MIMI. *(cont.)* This was the first one. That I fell in love with. Just a schoolgirl's parsed sentence, "The stagecoach shall depart at noon." An ordinary event in 1863. No name, just a young girl writing out a sentence for her grammar class two centuries back. I found it in an old book, and when I held it – there was this immediate connection – the flow of the ink in a particular slant, something about how mundane it was, mundane but something someone had thought to save. When I held it it was as if I knew her. Like I could feel from the ink her hand, and from her hand her wrist, her arm, her mind, her soul…I conjured her from this one piece of paper.

*(**MIMI** hands **KAI** the document. He takes it carefully.)*

KAI. It's…evidence, I guess. Evidence of a life, an ordinary life.

MIMI. A young girl standing on the side of a dusty road, waiting to begin a journey.

*(**KAI** hands back the document. They take great care with it. **MIMI** goes to put it away.)*

It isn't worth anything; I couldn't even sell it for the price of a plain frame– but I love this one most of all.

(standing apart still:)

I gave him his chair back.

KAI. It wasn't a bad chair.

MIMI. You hated it.

KAI. Yeah.

(They take each other in uncertainly from a small distance. Lights fade out.)

End of Play

ABOUT THE AUTHOR

NEENA BEBER's plays include *Jump/Cut, A Common Vision, The Dew Point, Hard Feelings* (Ojai Playwrights Conference), *Tomorrowland* (New Gorges; Theatre J in Washington D.C.), *Failure to Thrive, The Course of It, The Brief but Exemplary Life of the Living Goddess* (Magic Theatre) and *Misreadings* (ATL's Humana Festival, published in *The Best American Short Plays 1997*). *Thirst,* commissioned by Otterbein College, has been developed in The Public Theatre's New Work Now, Seattle's ACT, Williamstown Theatre Festival, and HBO's Stage to Screen. Other plays have premiered at Padua Playwrights Festival, circus minimus, Soho Rep, Watermark Theatre, En Garde Arts, and City Theatre, among other places. A.S.K. Exchange to the Royal Court Theatre, Distinguished Alumni Award from NYU's Tisch School of the Arts, member of New Dramatists. Short film: *Bad Dates,* based on her one act *Fool.* She has received Emmy and Ace-Award nominations for her writing for television, and has contributed plays to the 52nd Street Project. She is the recipient of Paulette Goddard and MacDowell Colony Fellowships.

From the Reviews of
THE DEW POINT...

"...A comedy of sexual manners whose characters are funny
yet sympathetic and complexly believable...The success of this
deceptively labeled "romantic comedy" lies in the way it zeroes in
on the way we deceive others by deceiving ourselves, plumping the
bread of friendship into some pretty rancid sandwiches that are, of
course, proffered with the best of intentions."
– Carolyn Clay, *Boston Phoenix*

"It is a pleasure to report that *The Dew Point* by Neena Beber, who
won a *Village Voice* OBIE last season for emerging playwright, is
an intelligent, well constructed, contemporary drama with sharp,
bright, witty dialogue and fully detailed vibrant, believeable
characters."
– Bob Rendell, *Talkin' Broadway*

Also by
Neena Beber...

A Common Vision

Jump/Cut

Tomorrowland

Please visit our website **samuelfrench.com** for complete
descriptions and licensing information.

OTHER TITLES AVAILABLE FROM SAMUEL FRENCH

TOMORROWLAND
Neena Beber

Dramatic Comedy / 3m, 4f

Anna has left graduate school to join the real world, as a writer on a children's television show in Orlando, Florida, she finds that world to be more surreal and absurd than anything she's left behind.

Tomorrowland takes a darkly comic look at death, Disney, and the search for meaning in a world that worships the young and the fake.

"Briskly hilarious comedy about a brittle New Yorker who abandons her doctoral dissertation on Virginia Woolf's use of parenthesis to write scripts for kid's TV show."
– Bob Mondello, *Washington City Paper*

"If you are not already terrified by the prospect of the Disneyfication of America, this wry exploration of its possible effects will put the fear of Mickey in you."
– Charlie Whitehead, *Time Out*